PAINTINGS, PUPPIES & MURDER

A Dickens & Christie Mystery

Book XII

Kathy Manos Penn

Paperback ISBN: 979-8-9887177-8-2

eBook ISBN: 979-8-9887177-7-5

Large Print ISBN: 979-8-9887177-9-9

Contents

CHAPTER ONE

THE SIGHT OF THE golden stone wall stretching into the distance took my breath away. I had perused the website extensively, but neither the description nor the photos of Foxbourne Park did it justice.

A stone wall also fronted Astonbury Estate, home to my friend Ellie, Dowager Countess of Stow, but it paled in comparison to this. Built of the same honey-colored Cotswold limestone, it bordered only a small part of the estate. What I was seeing now seemed to go on forever.

Finally, Wendy broke the silence. "I thought Astonbury Estate was large, but this place? Just how big is it?"

"The website said 400 acres, but since that's pretty much meaningless to me, I looked up New York City's Central Park to get an idea. If you can believe it, Foxbourne Park is nearly half the size of Central Park. That's pretty darned big. Dickens will be able to wander to his heart's content."

Dickens responded with a joyful bark. "I can't wait."

Approaching a T-junction, I slowed and turned right onto another narrow country lane. The wall continued uninterrupted on our right. I glimpsed several structures behind it but couldn't make out what they were. Further along on the left, sheep grazed in a pasture.

"That must be the entrance up ahead," said Wendy. "See the tall columns with the lanterns on top?"

I made the turn and stopped to take in the view of the tree-lined drive. "Those trees are massive. The website said they've been here since the 1600s, but I had no idea how huge they were."

"They're yew trees, like the ones around the door at St. Edward's Church in Stow. Except those two couldn't expand like the ones here. Instead, they grew around the door like a frame."

"Right. The image supposedly gave Tolkien the inspiration for the entrance to Moria in *The Lord of the Rings*. I wonder what this avenue of trees would have made him think of. They're not nearly as tall as oaks, but their spread is amazing. Just imagine, if they've been here for 400 years, they must have been planted thirty to forty feet apart."

It felt as though we'd entered another world, one that conjured up images of nuns or monks in silent contemplation. Rolling down my window, I drew in a deep breath. "If the manor house and grounds are this serene, you should be able to get plenty of writing done."

Wendy cut her eyes at me. "I told you. I'm taking a break. My plan is to let the book simmer, as you would say, and take a fresh look at it when we get back to Astonbury. If an idea about the problematic confrontation scene comes to me while we're here,

I'll write it out in longhand. But that's as close as I plan to come to writing."

We had attended a writers' retreat in October, and each of us had started a book. Our plan was to write murder mysteries instead of getting tangled up in them. Why that didn't work out could be the subject of yet another book. Still, since then, we'd been on the straight and narrow.

Because I was in the midst of planning a wedding, I'd given myself special dispensation to set aside my book. It was much more fun to shop for a wedding dress and ponder the perfect time and place for our nuptials than to write a murder mystery. Ellie had offered her home for the ceremony, and Dave and I had explored venues in Cornwall in October, but we hadn't decided yet.

The first hurdle had been fending off my sisters' suggestions that I return to Atlanta to get married. Neither of them could accept that Astonbury was my home now, and that I wanted to marry either in the UK or somewhere on the Continent. Dave and I hadn't ruled out a destination wedding in Greece or France. We agreed that the decision about the locale would dictate the timing, and being open to endless possibilities was both exciting and overwhelming.

Dickens stuck his head over my shoulder and sniffed. "I smell horses, Leta."

As I proceeded up the drive, I reminded Wendy about the amenities at Foxbourne Park. "With the stables, the spa, the pond, and goodness knows what else, this promises to be the grandest vacation I've had in ages. I still can't believe Ellie's generosity."

Wendy pulled out her copy of the invitation Ellie had given us for Christmas. "I know. We never exchange more than plates of biscuits for the holidays, so this gift came out of the blue. Mum says it's because we've given Ellie a new lease on life. She was in danger of becoming a recluse after the earl died. Instead, she and Mum are traveling and enjoying life to the max."

"True. She was quick to remind me that attending a yoga retreat in Tintagel and a literary conference in Torquay would never have entered her mind if not for us. Heck, she and your mum enjoyed Knight's Rest so much, they went back to Cornwall for another week of yoga in September."

Remembering how Belle eagerly set aside her cane to do chair yoga made me smile. Our local instructor, Rhiannon, had been behind that first trip and had also convinced Gemma to join us. It was rare that the prickly detective inspector took any extended time off, and a week of yoga was just what she needed—not to mention the visit resulted in a long-distance romance with a local DI.

The week before Christmas, Ellie had invited the five of us plus our friend Libby to lunch at the manor house and presented us with envelopes tied with red velvet ribbons. When we opened them, confetti spilled out, and we erupted in gasps of delight.

It was Belle who spoke up first. "Foxbourne Park! You're treating us to a stay at Foxbourne Park? Ellie, this is too much."

"Rubbish, Belle. Lavinia Foxbourne and I have been friends forever. I intended for this to be my treat, but when I called to book a two-night visit for January, she came back with a stunning suggestion. What's the word? Comping? Lavinia is *comping* an additional three nights in exchange for our feedback about the updates to the estate prior to its grand reopening in March.

We'll be the first guests to sample the new menu, stay in the refurbished guest rooms, and enjoy the expanded spa offerings."

It was a shame Libby was missing the excursion. Ellie had especially chosen January for our girls' getaway, knowing the Olde Mill Inn would be closed that month. As it turned out, Libby had called Ellie later to beg off because January was paint and polish time at the inn.

I was replaying the luncheon in my head when Wendy grasped the dashboard. "Would you look at that?"

Out of nowhere, a man on horseback appeared, cantering down the middle of the avenue. He reined in his horse and dismounted by my window in one fluid move. Placing a gloved hand on the roof of the car, he peered in. "Who have we here? The rest of Lady Stow's entourage?"

"If that means the others beat us here, then yes, we're it."

When Wendy and I introduced ourselves, he doffed his cap and bowed. "Edward Foxbourne at your service, ladies. You go on ahead, and I'll follow to help with your bags."

Wendy turned in her seat to glance behind us as I drove on. "Leta, is Edward the viscount or is he the son? And my goodness, did you see those blue eyes?"

"A handsome viscount helping carry our bags would be something, wouldn't it? That may still happen, but Edward looks to be our age. That's too old to be the viscount's son. St. John Foxbourne is the viscount and he's sixtyish, so his son can't be in his fifties. I remember the name because I've always been struck by how you Brits pronounce it. I would say 'Saint John'—not Sinjin."

"And yet, as a last name or as the name of a place, we say it like you do. I wonder whether the family will be as informal as Ellie. She can't stand for us to refer to her as Lady Stow."

In the distance, I glimpsed a large building of golden stone combined with brick. It wasn't Blenheim Palace by any means, but it was easily twice the size of Ellie's manor house. With its gables, turrets, and towers, it was similar in style to Stanway House, the home where J.M. Barrie and his author friends had often summered. We had toured it as a group as part of Dave's book launch.

I pulled in beside Ellie's Bentley. "Wendy, how many people do you think it takes to run this place? I imagine the staff parking is hidden somewhere."

"The website said the family is involved in the running of it, but they must have a kitchen staff and maids."

Suddenly, Edward was once again by my car window. "If you'll open the boot, I'll retrieve your bags." He opened my door and offered his hand to help me. With a grin, he motioned to Dickens. "Shall I let the dog out, too?"

Why did he look familiar to me? As I took in the broad shoulders and the blond curls touching his collar, it hit me. If he were dressed for a fox hunt, he could easily have graced the cover of a romance novel.

The front door was flung wide as we started up the stairs, and we were greeted by a younger man who bore a faint resemblance to Edward. He had the same blue eyes and build, but his dark hair was shorter. "Welcome. I'm Sebastian or Bash, whichever you prefer. And this must be the famous hero dog, Dickens."

That's all it took for Dickens to sit by his feet and yip. "That's me. Do you have treats?"

I held out my hand. "I see his reputation has preceded him. Yes, this is the hero dog, and I'm his personal servant, Leta Parker."

As Wendy introduced herself, Edward nodded toward the curving grand staircase in the lobby and carried our bags beyond it toward the hall. "I'll deliver these to your rooms while Bash escorts you via the scenic route."

Bash grinned. "Most guests prefer to take the stairs, at least when they first arrive. Others take one look and head for the elevator."

Winking at me, Wendy tilted her head. "Let me guess. Ellie climbed the stairs, but my mum used the elevator."

"If you mean Mrs. Davies, I can assure you she wanted to follow Lady Stow, but common sense prevailed."

Hearing someone clear their throat, I looked up to see Belle standing at the upstairs railing. "It's a beautiful staircase, isn't it? Now, hurry, you two. We're being escorted on a tour of the grounds before tea."

Another face peered down from the landing. "Hello. I'm Lavinia Foxbourne. No need to rush. Let Bash show you to your rooms and then meet us in the courtyard. Be sure to dress warmly, as we'll walk a bit."

Retrieving our room keys from the front desk, tucked in an alcove to the left of the stairs, Bash led the way. Upstairs, Rhiannon exited her room as we walked down the hall. "Wait until you see your rooms. I'm told they're all luxurious but with different decorative touches. Don't make the mistake of lying on the bed even for a minute, or you won't want to get up."

Bash smiled knowingly. "That's what we like to hear. I predict you'll have the same reaction. Here you go, Miss Davies." Stopping at a room with a brass plaque that read Rose Boudoir, he opened the door to a room painted in soft pink.

Wendy squealed and pointed to the bed before taking in the artwork. "I love the rose damask comforter and the white furniture. And, goodness, the artwork sets it off perfectly." She approached a grouping on the side wall. "Are these Mary Delaney collages? Surely, they're reproductions."

"Good eye, Miss Davies. Yes, these are prints. Most of the original collages hang in the British Museum."

"Leta, she should be an inspiration to us. She began crafting collages at age 72 and produced nearly a thousand in ten years. We may be getting a late start on our writing, but surely, we can publish a cozy mystery or two."

The lifelike flowers made me want to reach out and touch them. "I've never heard of her, but now that I have, I'd love to have a set of her prints for my office. And you're right, she's an inspiration."

With Dickens at our heels, Bash and I left Wendy unzipping her suitcase. He led the way down the hall past several more rooms and an elevator until we reached an archway on the left. It was little more than a deep alcove, holding an ornate door with large brass hinges and studs. Tugging a round oversized key ring from his pocket, Bash unlocked it to reveal a staircase lit by wall sconces. "After you, Miss Parker."

I felt like the damsel in a gothic novel, one about to be locked away in the tower.

CHAPTER TWO

BASH MUST HAVE SENSED my hesitation. "Lady Stow didn't have any instructions regarding the other guests, but she specially requested this room for you. I think you'll understand why when you see it."

Curving to the right, the stairway ended at a landing. I glimpsed what I thought was an elevator behind a curtain before my eyes landed on a colorful bouquet on a table by a second door. A small brass plaque read The Amethyst Retreat.

Bash unlocked the door and ushered me inside. The room was warm and elegant, with walls painted in a soft, dusky purple accented by ivory trim. The canopy bed, draped in sheer plum-colored gauze, boasted a deep amethyst velvet coverlet over crisp white linens. An assortment of embroidered pillows in various shades of violet and lilac added a touch of opulence.

The furniture was vintage, its white-painted wood upholstered in striped amethyst and ivory fabric. A plush Aubusson rug in muted purples and creams softened the polished wood floor. Opposite the bed, a fireplace sat flanked by two inviting, overstuffed armchairs in rich mulberry, with a neatly stacked pile of logs ready to be lit.

As my gaze drifted to the French doors draped in flowing ivory sheers, Bash crossed the room to unlock them.

"Oh my gosh, what a peaceful view," I murmured as I stepped outside. An expansive terraced lawn, dotted with towering oaks, led to a large pond with a gazebo on its far side. The balcony, complete with two cushioned chaise lounges and an iron bistro table, was the perfect place to take it all in.

"In warmer weather, guests often have their morning coffee or evening cocktails out here. Now, let me show you what I consider the pièce de résistance, and I'll be on my way." He led me to the far side of the room.

For a moment, I thought we'd entered the spa. Twin vanities framed the entrance to a luxurious bathroom, where an oversized soaking tub took center stage against the far wall, flanked by flickering candles and trailing greenery in delicate wall niches. A folding screen to the left featured three mirrored panels, and a walk-in shower with gleaming tiles occupied the right side.

"Bash, is this perchance the honeymoon suite?"

"It certainly is. Does it meet with your approval, Miss Parker?"

"Bash, it's Leta, and yes, it certainly does. I may never leave my room."

He'd no sooner departed than I heard the rumble of the elevator followed by a knock. It was Edward with my luggage. As he set my bags on the chest at the foot of the bed, he winked. "I hope you enjoy your stay, though it seems a shame to be on your own in the honeymoon suite."

I held up my left hand. "Who knows? I may return with my fiancé."

When he left, I took a video of the Amethyst Retreat and sent it to Dave. "I'm in the honeymoon suite."

An immediate response popped up. "Alone, I hope."

"For the moment."

When my phone played its Billy Joel ring tone, I knew it was Dave. "For the moment? Is that an invitation? I can pack up Christie and be right there, you know."

Christie meowed in the background. "Tell him to forget it, Leta. I'm not leaving my spot in front of his stove."

"Okay, tell me what she said. She's in her basket here in my shed, and she looks pretty comfy."

Until late last year, no one had known that I spoke to the animals—literally. This strange talent was something I'd had since I was a child, and had kept hidden until Dave moved in.

When I finally told him, I watched him progress from amusement at my joking to concern that I was delusional, though he was smart enough not to utter that word. Dickens and I convinced him with a demonstration, and the more he learned, the more delighted he was.

"She says she's not budging. I guess Dickens and I will have to make do here on our own. Apparently, Ellie arranged for me to have this room. I think she's trying to help me decide about the wedding venue, the honeymoon, or both."

"You'll know it when you see it, Leta. It's fun exploring options, and I'm happy to wait until you find the perfect spot. Ruling out the States was a start."

"Your patience is one of the many reasons I love you, Dave Prentiss. Now, I've got to run. We're taking a tour of the estate. Film at eleven."

Dickens and I were the last ones to make it outside, where two golf carts awaited us. Belle, Gemma, and Wendy climbed into the first one, driven by Lavinia Foxbourne. Edward was the driver of the second golf cart, and Ellie sat in the front seat next to him, her legs wrapped in a blanket. Rhiannon motioned me to the second row with her, which left the rear-facing last seat for Dickens. I was glad I'd worn layers, a scarf, and my favorite black cloche.

Edward began the tour with a description of Foxbourne Hall's origins as we sat in front of the manor house. When King James I granted 400 acres to Sir Reginald Foxbourne in the early 1600s, Sir Reginald started construction on a Jacobean manor house. That original home was approximately 12,000 square feet. It was the second Sir Reginald who was given the title Viscount Foxbourne in 1688.

Sitting so that he could address all three of us, Edward explained he was named for Viscount Edward Foxbourne, who, in the early 1700s, had embarked on a significant expansion of the manor. It grew to around 30,000 square feet, and it was then that the first formal gardens were added. "Leta," said the current-day Edward, "did you notice the maze from your balcony?"

"Yes. I thought that's what it was. How amazing to think the design is over three hundred years old."

"Mum will take you on a tour of the interior while you're here, but for now, we're going to follow the timeline and visit the gazebo." As we looped around the manor house, the gazebo I'd glimpsed from my balcony came into view.

"Viscount Henry Foxbourne, like many prominent landowners in the late 1700s, strove to beautify the estate—form over function, if you will. The gazebo on the edge of the pond came first, followed by the folly you see in the distance."

When we disembarked at the gazebo, Edward pointed out the columns and bench seats that lined its circumference. "In the warmer months, we add colorful hanging baskets and serve tea out here, but I'm afraid that's not an option in January."

I was surprised when we didn't turn toward the tower. "No tour of the folly?" I asked.

"Not until my brother has it repaired. It's no longer safe to climb, so we keep it locked. Did you think it would be like Broadway Tower?"

Ellie chuckled. "I know better, Edward. It's lovely from the outside, but even years ago, when Nigel and I occasionally climbed it with your parents, it held nothing more than a spiral, stone staircase. I remember it as dank and musty. Lovely view from the top, though."

"That's why our next stop will be the stables. They were added by my great-great-grandmother Eleanor in the Victorian era. Of course, she built them for the family horses, but now we keep enough animals to allow our guests to ride, too. I'd be delighted to take you ladies on a ride one morning while you're here, or several mornings if you like."

Rhiannon grimaced. "No thank you. I was thrown by a horse when I was a child, and I've never gotten on one since."

When Ellie demurred, Edward gave me an inquiring glance. "Don't look at me. I'm more a horse-drawn carriage kind of girl."

Wendy, Belle, and Gemma were entering the stables when we arrived, and Lavinia stood outside speaking with a woman with strawberry blonde hair. "Ladies," Lavinia called, "let me introduce you to Annabelle Thompson, our riding instructor."

"I'm afraid she's out of luck with this group," Edward said. "Not a rider among them."

Annabelle's high ponytail shook as she laughed. "You never know. If I can get you up on a gentle ride, you might enjoy at least walking the trails on horseback. If not, you're welcome to ply the gang with carrots."

I told her about my regular visits with the donkeys near my cottage. "Carrots are more my speed, and I'm sure Dickens would like to get to know the horses. Maybe we'll drop by tomorrow." She suggested I check with her dad, who was inside.

Before I knew it, Dickens disappeared into the stables. Inside, Belle was feeding carrots to a pale grey horse named Misty. "I'm told she's a Connemara pony, Leta."

Wendy waved me over to where she and Gemma were conferring with a man I took to be Annabelle's father. "Leta, I'm going horseback riding tomorrow. Haven't done that in ages, but Rob assures me it will come back to me and Misty will be a gentle ride. Rob, meet my friend Leta."

"Pleased to meet you, ma'am. If there's anything you need or any questions you have about our horses, please don't hesitate to ask."

"I just met your daughter. I won't be riding, but I'll drop by to hand out carrots and get to know the horses." I glanced at Gemma. "Will you be riding?"

"Maybe. It's been a while for me too. If I do, it will be more like ambling than anything else."

Dickens barked my name. "Leta, come meet Lucky and her puppies!"

I followed his voice to the far end of the stable, where a small, scruffy grey-and-white terrier mix stood proudly beside a bed of straw. Her coat was wiry, her ears half-flopped, and her dark button eyes studied me. When I crouched down beside her, she tentatively wagged her tail.

"Hi, Lucky. May I see your puppies?"

"If you don't wake them," she said, tipping her head.

I peered into the stall, where a nest of tiny, squirming puppies nestled in the straw. Their fur was a mix of black, white, and brown patches. Some were fast asleep, one let out a tiny yawn, and another gave a half-hearted wriggle before settling back down.

As I took in the tableau, Lucky questioned me. "Tell me about Dickens. He says he's a Great Pyrenees, but I'm not sure I believe him. He's awfully tiny."

Dickens huffed and tapped her playfully on the snout. "Hey, I'm bigger than you, and I'll have you know I'm a hero dog."

With a little huff of laughter, Lucky trotted outside with Dickens on her heels.

Speaking softly, Rhiannon joined me. "They're precious, aren't they? I just want to scoop one up." We reminisced about the time kittens had been born in the donkey barn. I'd toyed with the idea of adopting one, until Christie put her paw down. Rhiannon and my neighbors, the Watsons, went home with one each, so at least I got to visit them.

I left Rhiannon with the puppies and went in search of Dickens. Belle, Gemma, and Wendy had disappeared, and Ellie was conferring with Rob.

Outside, Edward and Annabelle stood with their heads together, deep in conversation. From the corner of the stables,

Dickens let out a playful bark. I found him rolling in the frost-covered grass with Lucky darting around him, her grey fur a cute contrast to his white.

"Are you having a good time, Dickens?" I asked.

"Oh yes," he said, panting. "Lucky says I should come back and play more."

Reaching down, I scratched Lucky under her chin. She leaned into my touch, tail wagging, and Dickens nudged her. "Go on, tell her your story."

A sad sigh came from the new mom. "My people left me behind when they moved away. It was warm then, so I slept under hedges and found scraps where I could, but I was always hungry."

Dickens barked knowingly. "I did that once with Buttercup. Remember, Leta?"

"How could I forget? You two took off, and I was frantic. You were darned lucky I found you."

Lucky's ears perked up at that. "That's what Rob said, too. One cold night, I followed the scent of hay and wandered into the stables. He gave me water, a warm bed, and my name." She nuzzled Dickens. "And I've been Lucky ever since."

Ellie was effusive about our next stop. "Nigel and I spent many a partridge season here, Edward. You know your father was a keen sportsman, and your mother still enjoys the hunt."

"I'd forgotten that, Lady Stow. When I was a boy, we had guests nonstop over hunting season. Of course, once I went away to school, I missed out on that. And I mostly lived on the Continent as an adult. Even now, I'm merely passing through."

"I'm sure your presence is appreciated, what with the grand reopening on the horizon. How long do you plan to be here?"

"I assured St. John and Charlotte I'd stay through early April. Then, I'm off to parts unknown." Pulling up to the hunting lodge, he spoke to Rhiannon and me. "Ladies, Ellie knows all this, but the lodge was added in the early 1900s by our great-grandfather."

"Perhaps Lavinia and I can spend a few pleasant hours shooting if the weather holds," Ellie said. "I brought my shotgun."

Chuckling, I tapped her on the shoulder. "Is that the same gun you brought when you scared the bejeezus out of that dognapper?"

"It certainly is."

A choking sound came from Edward. "Sounds like a story we need to hear, perhaps over dinner."

Our last stop was the new barn, or as Edward described it, "St. John's latest brainchild." The viscount had it built as an events venue the year before, and it was already booked solid for this spring and summer.

Made of newer, lighter wood, it was an inviting structure, and the interior was a surprise. "Oh, my goodness. This place is stunning. It's overcast and growing dark outside, but the lighting in here is bright and cheery. And it's somehow rustic yet modern."

"You can credit Charlotte for that," said Edward. "You'll meet her at cocktails, and she'll be happy to regale you with the special touches she used. Those lights in the vaulted ceiling? She calls them fairy lights, but they provide an enormous amount of illumination. The hay bales are a decorative touch for now, but when they're removed, the whole place has a more elegant look."

Ellie watched me as I turned in a circle. "Do you like it, Leta?"

"Yes. It has a fairy-tale vibe—like something out of a Disney movie."

"Perhaps the perfect spot for a fairy-tale wedding?"

As I nodded, I heard Dave's words. "You'll know it when you see it, Leta."

CHAPTER THREE

BASH AND TWO WOMEN awaited us at the front door of the manor house. Jogging down the stairs, he joined his uncle in assisting us from the golf carts before the two drove them away.

The older woman stepped forward. "Good afternoon. I'm Charlotte Foxbourne, and this is my daughter Emilia." Ushering us inside, they took our coats and scarves and pointed the way to the drawing room for afternoon tea.

A petite woman with brown eyes and a button nose, Charlotte wore her blonde hair in a loose chignon at the nape of her neck. Emilia could have been her twin but for her green eyes. She too had blonde hair, though hers hung in soft waves below her shoulders.

Rhiannon and I made a beeline for the beverage table with its variety of teas. Sparkling wine was also an option, but what I wanted most was a hot drink. Cups in hand, we moved to one of the small round tables arranged by the bay window.

"I adore afternoon tea," said Rhiannon. "If someone would deliver a selection like this to my flat every afternoon, I'd be in heaven."

"It makes your vegetarian heart sing, doesn't it?" The tiered tray had yummy-looking sandwiches on the bottom—cucumber, egg salad, and smoked salmon—and scones with cream and jam, and a variety of cakes and pastries on top. The comments from the other tables told me she wasn't alone.

As Rhiannon nodded and bit into a finger sandwich, Emilia joined us. "I hope you enjoyed the tour, despite the chill."

"Absolutely. I never cease to be fascinated with the history here in England. Imagine being able to trace your family line back to the 1600s. I know both my grandfathers emigrated from Greece in the early twentieth century, but that's about it."

Rhiannon chose another sandwich. "I'm looking forward to yoga in the barn tomorrow morning. Ellie tells me your mother wants my input on how well the space will work for classes. Will you be joining us, Emilia?"

"Yes, we both plan to be there. Our only concern is whether it will be warm enough, given the high ceiling. If it works in January, it should be fine pretty much all year long." She winked. "I'm looking forward to having a real live yoga instructor. Since I moved home from London, I've been making do with YouTube videos."

Studying the array of delicacies on the tiered tray, I chose a miniature éclair. "Edward mentioned the barn was booked through the summer. What kinds of events are you hosting?"

"As we expected, weddings are by far the most popular. We've got a Spring Ball and a retirement party in the mix—and a few birthday parties, too. Bash handles bookings and is always happy to provide color commentary on what that's like."

She glanced at my éclair and put one on her plate. "My forte is the spa. I own several day spas in London and presented a business case to Dad about adding one here. The numbers suited him, so here I am. I was delighted to see that all six of you have signed up for treatments this week."

Rhiannon rotated her neck and shoulders. "I'm on the schedule for a massage tomorrow."

"That means you'll meet Sophie. She was my most sought-after massage therapist in London, and she's developed quite a clientele here among the locals. It was quite a coup to entice her down from London. We also acquired a microderm machine in October. Mum's a convert."

"Since I haven't convinced Rhiannon to offer massage in her studio in Astonbury, I signed up to get one here first thing. Now that I know you offer microderm, I'll plan on that too."

It was my job to write about Foxbourne Park as a destination, and I saw my spa experience as the topic of at least one column. I had no plans to experience horseback riding or hunting, but interviews with Wendy and Ellie would give me what I needed about those activities. My firsthand accounts of the spa, the food, and the ambience were sure to be of interest to my readers—those in the Cotswolds and in the States.

When my phone pinged with a text from Dave, I laughed and showed it to my tablemates. "Dave can't figure out what Christie wants. He sent a video of her in his face talking to him."

Rhiannon rolled her eyes. "Does he honestly think any of us know what our cats want? Snowball's like Christie, quite vocal and demanding." She pulled out her phone and showed Emilia her white cat. "Christie and Snowball join us for cat yoga at least once a week."

Excusing myself, I turned up the sound on the video as I walked to my room. I waited until I propped myself up on the bed before calling Dave with the answer to his question. "She quite clearly said, 'Feed me,' several times, followed by 'What part of feed me wet food do you not get?' She seems quite put out with you." It was all I could do to keep a straight face as I explained this to him.

"How was I supposed to know that? We're in the shed, and it's not anywhere near dinnertime. She cried at the door. I let her out. She cried on the other side. I let her in. I gave her treats, and she turned her nose up at them."

Christie meowed, "He needs you, Leta. We both do."

That cracked me up. "Oh, puhleeze, Christie. You two don't need me. You're just being a pain. Now hush. I'm sending Dave something."

I texted the video of the barn. "Tell me what you think."

He was much better at reading me than understanding Christie. "Nice! Does this mean you've found it? The place for our wedding?"

"I think so. Like you said, I knew it as soon as I saw it. It will work in any season, and the manor house has twenty guest rooms, more than enough for friends and family from the States."

"You talked about a Christmas wedding, but we couldn't pull that off fast enough for this past December. Is that what you want?"

"Yes. If not around Christmas, I'll take fall. Imagine the colorful leaves. Either way, I think it's perfect."

Dickens and I indulged in a brief nap before I dressed for cocktails. Content to loll by the fire, he watched as I did my fluff and dust routine. Fluff my hair with the blow dryer, reapply makeup, and add a touch of dusting powder before getting dressed.

I chose a black satin tank top and fitted burgundy jacket to top my wide-legged black pants. *Perfect*, I thought, as I added the gold chain with the tear-shaped garnet stone. After a spritz of Shalimar, I slipped my feet into my black heels and twirled in front of the folding mirror.

"Dickens, you look smashing in your black bow tie. What do you say I let you out and then you escort me to cocktails?"

He barked in enthusiastic agreement, and we rode the elevator down. "Don't be long," I said as he darted down the steps. My burgundy jacket wasn't made to ward off the chilly night air, and I wasn't about to spoil the look with a hooded coat.

We were back inside in time to see Gemma descending the stairs. She'd traded her ponytail for a becoming topknot and wore a forest green tunic over brown pants. It was nice to see her in something other than running clothes or a dark suit. "Don't you look lovely, Gemma? I'm so glad you were able to get the week off."

"Thanks, Leta. I really need this break. I'm worn out from the long hours over the holidays and traveling back and forth to see Jake."

"And how is Jake? Did you two get to celebrate Christmas or ring in the New Year together?" Her scowl told me that was a sore subject.

"Let's just say we were in the same place, but there wasn't much celebrating. And before you ask, it's the usual. Crime never takes a break."

I looped my arm in hers. "Sounds like you could use a cocktail." According to the itinerary slipped beneath my door, the study did double duty as the bar. The room was open to guests all day but only served drinks during the lunch hour and again in the evening.

At the door, Gemma whispered in my ear, "Looks like we're the last to arrive."

Our group had already made themselves comfortable in the inviting wood-paneled room. Holding elegant martini glasses, Wendy and Rhiannon stood at the bar chatting with Edward. Belle sat on a loveseat with Lavinia, and Bash had Ellie and Emilia in stitches in front of the fireplace.

I joined Charlotte at the far end of the bar. "What a lovely room. Has it only recently doubled as a bar?"

"Yes. We made room for it two years ago. It was either that or employ more staff to ferry drinks back and forth. This way, we can have one person behind the bar part-time, and a convenient buzzer for off hours, if a guest is in need of a drink."

Charlotte looked over my shoulder. "St. John, come meet Leta Parker. She's Ellie's friend who's writing about Foxbourne Park."

Turning, I saw a distinguished gentleman. Like his brother, St. John was tall with broad shoulders. His dark hair tinged with grey gave him a more commanding presence than Edward. I knew from Ellie that he had started and sold several successful businesses and was still involved in at least one.

He shook my hand before leaning in to peck Charlotte's cheek. "Sorry, luv, the meeting ran over, but I'm happy to say it went well." He tilted his head. "I see you're wearing your emerald choker, but where are the earrings?"

Charlotte touched her ear. "They're just a bit ornate for tonight. I think these small gold ones work better with my outfit."

Her comment reminded me of a fun outing with my Atlanta girlfriends years ago. "Goodness, Charlotte, you've triggered a flashback." I described Style Camp, a Saturday seminar that helped us identify the styles that worked best with our shapes, coloring, and lifestyle. I was encouraged to wear more scarves and to indulge my love of hats. "One thing that stuck with me was the tip that wearing matching jewelry was no longer the thing. The instructor called it *matchy-matchy*, and declared the look taboo."

"That's it, Leta. The earrings and the necklace together are just too much, especially in this day and age."

St. John rolled his eyes. "That distinction is beyond me, ladies. Now, we must get you a drink, Leta. Edward's a dab hand at martinis, but of course, we also have wine."

A vision of the barn flashed into my head. "It's rare I drink a martini, but I'd love a French 75 if Edward's willing. I'm in the mood to celebrate."

Gemma came up behind me. "Ditto to a French 75. Now tell us what you're celebrating, Leta."

"An important decision." I felt a grin spread across my face. "I've been agonizing over where to get married, and today, I fell in love with the barn. I want to get married there."

With a wink, St. John called down the bar. "Edward, we're celebrating. These two ladies want French 75s, and I'll have my usual, thank you." He turned back to me. "We'd be delighted to host your nuptials, Leta. Do you have a date in mind?"

Out of the corner of my eye, I caught a flurry of activity at the other end of the bar. It was like a ripple effect. Ellie, Lavinia, and Belle came to stand behind me as a cork popped. Emilia and Bash ferried champagne flutes as Edward filled them.

When everyone had glasses, Wendy raised hers high. "Congratulations to our favorite couple. We finally know where the wedding will be!"

I blushed as laughter and cheers greeted her toast. Ellie asked the obvious question. "Have you settled on a date?"

I shared my Christmas idea, and Bash ducked from the room, saying he'd check the schedule. I groaned when Edward handed me my martini. "If I'd known champagne was on the way, I wouldn't have ordered this. I'll be worthless tomorrow if I keep this up."

Wendy put her arm around me. "You only live once, Leta. Enjoy yourself."

When Bash returned, he was smiling. "Leta, you're spoiled for choice for the barn and guest rooms, as long as you don't need all twenty. Christmas falls on a Wednesday this year. Do you prefer the Saturday before or the one after? I can manage fifteen rooms including the honeymoon suite both weeks."

I pulled out my phone. "Hold on. I should let Dave weigh in on this."

When he answered, I dove right in. "I'm in the bar with all of our friends, and I've got great news. We can have a December wedding—here at Foxbourne Park."

A soft chuckle came down the line. "You didn't waste any time, did you, sweetheart? It's a good thing my calendar is open."

"Very funny. The barn is ours and we have a choice of weeks." We discussed the pros and cons. It was high season for cross-Atlantic flights for our stateside guests, no matter which week we chose.

"Then, it's an easy decision for me, Leta. I say the weekend after so we can fly out on the twenty-ninth for our honeymoon. Destination TBD, of course. I can see it now, Paris or Venice or the Swiss Alps. How does that sound to you?"

"Perfect. I can't wait to start planning. You know I'll get plenty of input from the gang." With any luck, I'd arrive home with menu options and other items for Dave to consider. "Love you. Talk later."

Ellie hugged me. "I had my fingers crossed the combination of the Lavender Loft and the barn would do the trick. My work is done."

When Emilia led the way to the dining room, I stationed Dickens by the fireplace before following her. I was in time to hear her introduce an auburn-haired woman of about her age. "Ladies, this is Sophie Green, who works in the spa. Since we're running with a skeleton staff this month, she's kindly agreed to assist me in serving dinner tonight. Tomorrow evening, you'll be at Bash's mercy."

The dining room held tables of varying sizes, the largest one a rectangular table for ten. Tonight, there were twelve for dinner, as the Foxbourne family was dining with us. We made our way to two round tables and located our place cards. The three Foxbourne men pulled out our chairs as Sophie and Emilia offered wine.

Belle and Ellie shared a table with Charlotte, St. John, and Lavinia, with a place setting open for Emilia. Bash and Edward joined the rest of us.

Scanning our table, Edward winked. "Bash, my boy, I think we've snagged the best table in the house." He lifted his wineglass. "Ladies, may your stay be everything you want it to be."

As we lifted our glasses in response, Edward studied my right hand. "Leta, what an exquisite ring. Garnets of that size are rare, and the square cut shows it off to perfection."

"Thank you. It's always been one of my favorite pieces."

Wendy smiled at me. "Do you want to tell him the story of how you thought you'd lost it, or shall I?"

I gave her the go-ahead, and she shared the tale of Dave *borrowing* my ring as a prelude to his marriage proposal. He'd taken it so he could have his mother's engagement ring sized to fit me, and I'd gone a week thinking I'd lost it.

She pointed to my necklace. "He made up for it with a storybook proposal and then a garnet necklace for Christmas."

"Sounds like quite a guy. If I'm back at Christmas, I'll have to meet him," said Edward.

I missed his explanation about his holiday plans as I read the menu that lay atop my napkin. If tonight's selection was anything to judge by, we were in for a tasty week. The Taste of the Cotswolds selection included asparagus soup, roast lamb, and one of my favorite desserts, sticky toffee pudding.

Rhiannon, our lone vegetarian, was the only one to choose the Wild Mushroom and Spinach Wellington over the Braised Cotswold Lamb with Redcurrant & Rosemary. I nudged Wendy, who sat on my right. "I'll have to warn Dave that I'll be serving low-cal meals for at least a week once I get home. He needs to take advantage of my absence to eat burgers at the Ploughman with Peter."

"Since my brother is happy to eat burgers every night of the week, they'll be quite a pair. If he didn't cycle every day, he'd be as big as a house." I could count on Peter to ride by my cottage most mornings, and we cycled together on Sundays, weather permitting.

Seated on my left, Bash picked up on the mention of bicycles, and we launched into a discussion of cycling vacations. He was an engaging conversationalist, a plus in his role. He made it a point to invite Rhiannon's thoughts, and the talk turned to the benefits of yoga.

I turned the other way to find Wendy and Edward with their heads together. When Gemma caught my eye, she tilted her head toward the duo and rolled her eyes.

Sophie had taken our entrée orders, and now she served the starters. By this point, Edward had his hand on Wendy's arm. *Is this innocent flirting or flirting with intent?* He made no attempt to bring Gemma into the conversation. Had I missed a rebuff on her part, or was he totally taken with Wendy? For that matter, Wendy hadn't looked my way in ten minutes. *Odd.*

The rest of us moved from topic to topic, as happens over a meal. When I asked Gemma about riding the next day, she said she was looking forward to an afternoon outing with Annabelle. "I've got a full day planned. Yoga with Rhiannon, a massage with Sophie, and then riding after lunch. And I brought that book you recommended, the first in the Cormoran Strike series."

"Oh yes. I'm addicted to that series, and I've gotten Dave hooked on them, too. I can't wait to hear what you think, since Strike's a private investigator."

That got another Gemma eye roll. "But a licensed one, unlike some people I know, right?"

Since she'd added a smile to the eye roll, I chose not to let her remark get under my skin. I had to laugh when Rhiannon came to my defense. "Funny, isn't it, how effective unlicensed detectives can be?"

Bash looked from Gemma to Rhiannon with a puzzled look, but let the cryptic comments pass as Sophie arrived with our entrées. The enticing aroma of roast lamb pervaded the table, and a contented sigh passed my lips. "Goodness, how I love lamb, especially when someone else cooks it for me."

I was leaning back in my chair when I uttered those words, and I caught an exchange between Edward and Sophie. When she put his plate in front of him, he reached up, placed his hand on her upper arm, and whispered. Because she was looking down, I doubted anyone else observed her frown and shake her head. *People watching is endlessly entertaining.*

The room was noticeably quiet as we enjoyed our entrées. Even Wendy focused on her food rather than the man to her right. I leaned toward her. "How long's it been since you've seen Rhys?"

She pursed her lips. "Not since New Year's in London. Remember, he was supposed to come down in mid-January but had to cancel. The Golden Age Literary Association is taking more and more of his time this year. Something to do with adding a new sponsor."

The plan was for me to cook dinner for the four of us, but it turned out to be Wendy and her mum instead. Fine by me and Dave, but I knew Wendy had been disappointed. Dave and I had survived a lengthy cross-Atlantic relationship, so I didn't think much of Rhys's missed visit at the time. And since Dave's marriage proposal in September, Wendy and I had spent less time together. I needed to remedy that situation.

I hadn't noticed St. John was missing until he appeared in the doorway with a plump woman in an apron. I knew right away she had to be the person who had prepared our delectable dinner. "Allow me to introduce Edith Thompson, our chef. Edith, thank you for yet another mouthwatering meal."

As murmurs of appreciation sounded around the room, he put his arm around her waist. "I've already had a request for the asparagus soup recipe, and I imagine there will be similar requests as the week goes on."

"You know it's a pleasure, Lord Foxbourne."

He gave a hearty laugh. "Lord Foxbourne, indeed. I see you're on your best behavior." He looked around the room. "Would you believe we've known each other since we were children? Edith's father was our gamekeeper when I was a boy, and I remember her as a rambunctious toddler with a jam-smeared face."

With a toss of her head, Edith said, "You'd best take care if you're going to start sharing childhood memories. Who was it tempted me with the open jam jar?"

Edward chimed in. "Edith, I remember our toddler days, but my fondest memories are of riding horses together when we were teens. You met her daughter today. Annabelle's the spitting image of her mum."

Once he mentioned it, the likeness was obvious. Foxbourne Park was a family affair in more ways than one. The gamekeeper's daughter was married to the stable manager, and their daughter was the riding instructor. It put me in mind of Downton Abbey.

When the kitchen door opened, St. John and Edith made way for Emilia and Sophie carrying dessert. "That's quite enough about me," Edith said. "Enjoy your puddin', and I'll see you in the morning for breakfast." With that, she disappeared back into the kitchen.

We lingered over coffee and dessert, but soon folks began to take their leave. Belle and Ellie were the first to depart, followed by Rhiannon and Gemma. I was half expecting Wendy to suggest a nightcap, but instead she said she'd see me at breakfast before leaving with Edward. *Something is definitely amiss with her and Rhys.*

I was deep in thought when Sophie offered to top off my coffee. "Oh no," I said. "It's time I took my dog out and headed to bed."

As I pushed back my chair, Bash stood. "Leta, would you care to stop by the office after you walk Dickens? I can give you a brochure and menu options to look over."

"That's a grand idea. See you in a few minutes."

Much to Dickens's dismay, I shooed him down the front steps and told him to be quick. He was out and back in no time, and we found Bash behind the front desk. He opened a door to what he described as his coat closet of an office.

Laughing, I pointed to an array of coats hung on pegs. "You weren't kidding. It really *is* a coat closet."

"Everyone but me thinks this is the best spot so they're handy for guests who need an extra layer." He pointed to his left. "I've finally convinced Dad we can squeeze in an actual closet down the hall from the desk."

He walked me through the brochure and answered my random questions, from music options, to flowers, to the possibility of a local vicar if we wanted that kind of ceremony. "Leta, trust me. I can arrange pretty much anything you want. Talk to your fiancé and keep the questions coming."

Stifling a yawn, I gathered the brochures right as the door opened. It was Edward. "Oops. Didn't mean to interrupt. I need my coat." He reached behind me and was gone.

I couldn't help glancing at my watch, and Bash answered my unspoken question. "Uncle Edward likes his nightly walks. Not much else going on around here at nine thirty on a Sunday. I can recommend a few pubs in Deddington for later in the week, though." I assured him I'd be perfectly content here at Foxbourne Park.

Exiting the tiny office with Dickens, I was just in time to see Edward escorting Wendy out the front door. *A nightly walk or a night out?*

CHAPTER FOUR

NOT SURPRISINGLY, I WASN'T one bit hungry when I woke up the next day. I brewed coffee in the Nespresso machine hidden in the chifforobe and climbed back into bed to Google Christmas wedding ideas. A good morning text from Dave brought a smile to my face. It was a selfie of him in bed with Christie on his chest, so I sent him a pic of Dickens still sound asleep.

He rang right away. "So, what's on the agenda today?"

"A massage! I can't wait. And Dickens wants to see the horses and the puppies, so I'm sure we'll walk to the stables. How 'bout you? Since you're still in bed, I'm thinking you worked most of the night." Dave was a night owl, and it wasn't unusual for him to write into the wee hours.

"Yup. I put the finishing touches on Issa's article and will send it to the magazine today." We'd met the author at a writers' retreat in the fall, and she'd engaged Dave to interview her and write an article. We'd visited her and her son in Boston between Christmas and New Year's when we were in the States seeing our families.

"Now that it's done, I'm free to think of other things. Any guesses what they are?"

"Oh, let me think. Maybe honeymoon plans?"

"That's in the back of my mind, but right now, I'm thinking wedding music." Dave never ceased to amaze me. He was the most romantic man I'd ever met, but it hadn't occurred to me that he would weigh in on the music. I should have known better. "I think we need a piano player, maybe a guitar player too, and of course, a singer. What do you think of 'Till There Was You'? If not somewhere in the ceremony, at least for the reception."

"By the Beatles?"

"Well, yes, you love Paul McCartney's rendition, but you know the song is from *The Music Man*, right?"

"I had no idea. And I liked that movie, but it's '76 Trombones' that I remember. Is that it, or do you have more?"

"I'm not sure what you'll think of this, since this is your second wedding, but I'd really like to see you walk down the aisle to 'Here Comes the Bride.'"

"Of course, I'll do that! I love that you're thinking about music. As long as you don't decide on 'Brown-Eyed Girl' or something like that, we'll be fine." At heart, I was pretty traditional.

I let him go when Christie interrupted with a demand for food, and I turned to my easygoing dog. "Dickens, what do you say I shower and we take a walk?" His response was to yawn and roll over on his side. Clearly, there was no need for me to rush.

A perkier dog greeted me when I was ready, and he was raring to go when I pulled a ball from my suitcase. Outside, it was cloudy, but light enough for me to make my way to the gazebo. There wasn't a path per se, but a visible trail where others had walked. A heavy mist hung in the air as I threw the ball for Dickens and he romped back and forth.

"Leta, can we visit the puppies?"

"That's farther than I have time for this morning, Dickens. Let's do the gazebo for now, and I promise we'll see them after lunch."

My mind turned to wedding dresses as we strolled. Now that I knew it would be a winter wedding, I pictured a velvet dress in a rich burgundy or crimson—not fire-engine red, but something in the red family. And a fascinator of some sort.

As we approached the gazebo, I recognized the runner emerging from the mist. The lime green attire was a dead giveaway. "Running, yoga, a massage, and a horseback ride? Can you squeeze in anything else, Gemma?"

Laughing with pure joy, she put her hands on her knees. "If the weather clears, Ellie and I may do a bit of shooting before the sun sets. And Lavinia, too. You have no idea what a treat it is to have an entire week off—and in a setting like this." Waving, she took off around the pond.

I was happy to see Bash behind the desk. "Tell me you have some old, ragged towels. I can't possibly use the white ones in my room to dry Dickens."

"No worries." He pulled a fluffy brown towel from beneath the counter. "We aim to please all of our guests—both two- and four-legged."

In the dining room, the three senior ladies were indulging in a full English breakfast. "Join us, Leta," said Lavinia. "Those red cheeks tell me you've been out for a walk. I hope you've worked up an appetite."

I grabbed an apple from the breakfast bar and took a seat. The three wasted no time telling me I simply must have more than that.

"Not today. A full stomach doesn't work with a massage."

"That's why we're spacing out our activities," said Ellie. "We'll start with a leisurely stroll. After that, it's chair yoga with Rhiannon and free time until lunch. What we do this afternoon will depend upon the weather. We may go into Deddington."

When Rhiannon popped into the dining room in her yoga attire, she headed straight for the fruit bowl. "Good morning, ladies. Charlotte and Emilia have finished their yoga session, and Bash says he'll bring the golf cart around to the rear entrance when it's time for yours." She looked at Belle. "That way, you can avoid the steps."

I wondered aloud where Wendy was, and Belle said she'd found a note slipped beneath her door. "She and Edward are horseback riding. They had an early breakfast and were off with the sunrise, and Edith packed a lunch for them."

Thankfully, I managed not to choke on the bite of apple I'd just taken. *A full day of horseback riding? And not a word to me?* We two didn't live in each other's pockets, but on girls' trips, Wendy and I stuck together more often than not. This trip was odd because none of us were sharing rooms, but still.

I tuned back into the conversation around the table as Ellie mentioned St. John. "I remember him as the serious one, and it doesn't appear that's changed."

Lavinia concurred. "You're right, Ellie. His father used to say that everything St. John touched turned to gold, as though his business success came easily. I don't think he ever realized how hard his firstborn worked. St. John's always been driven, and it's only lately that he's slowed down a bit."

Buttering her toast, Ellie gave a knowing smile. "Edward's more like his father, isn't he?"

"There's no doubt about it. Edward inherited not only his looks, but also his penchant for the finer things in life. I don't know where St. John got his business sense, but it wasn't from his father."

"Lavinia," I said, "Edward mentioned he was only here for a short while. Where does he live?"

"That, my dear, is not a question with a simple answer. He and his wife split their time between her homes in Paris and Provence, but when she died, those went to the children from her first marriage. Edward's been a bit at loose ends since then. He may know where he'll land next, but he hasn't shared that with me."

Something about her answer told me there was more to Edward's story. Maybe Wendy would learn more today.

I followed the knee-high bronze signs that pointed the way to the rear of the carriage house. Goodness knew how many cars and carriages had been stored there before a portion of the two-story building had been turned into a spa. Even now, plenty of room remained for several autos.

Emilia greeted me at the door and took my coat. Today, she wore an elegant blush-colored ensemble. The long-sleeved, high-collared tunic top matched the fashionable pants with stovepipe legs. "Let me show you around before you change for your appointment with Sophie."

She'd painted three walls of the lobby a deep shade of blush, and textured floral wallpaper with hints of gold covered the fourth. When I commented on the pale hue of the wood floor, Sophie explained she had used oak boards, coated them in watery white paint, and wiped it off before it dried. The addition of plush cream-colored rugs provided a cozy feel.

Every element was rose, gold, or cream. The fabric on the overstuffed chairs was cream suede, and tall metallic vases filled with pale pink roses adorned an accent table against one wall. I admired the painting of a rose garden that hung above it, commenting that I liked the contrasting dark and light colors.

"Look closely and you'll see the signature, E. Fox. Uncle Edward painted it and the others around the room. These are some of his older pieces, the ones he painted when he was in his Mary Delaney phase." She drew my attention to the glass reception counter that displayed a collection of jewelry. "These are Sophie's designs, all made with semi-precious stones."

The designs were intriguing. Not all of the stones were familiar to me, but I recognized the hematite, the amethyst, and the garnet. I'd have to get Sophie to tell me the names of the others. There were also two carving sets and several daggers with bejeweled handles. I picked up one of the business cards on the counter. Centered on the front were the initials SEG in a simple black script. The top left corner featured three gemstones—amethyst, emerald, and sapphire—in a triangle pattern.

"Now, before I turn you over to Sophie, let me show you the other treatment rooms. Sophie's is strictly for massages, but these two are equipped for facials with magnifying lamps, facial steamers, and hot towel cabinets."

To the left of each door hung a small bronze plaque with the image of a rose. Opening the first door, she pointed out the equipment. "This one also has a high-frequency machine and our new microdermabrasion machine. Both Sophie and I are estheticians, so you can take your pick. I hope you'll make a facial appointment while you're here."

"I definitely will, and I might even indulge in a second massage."

Sophie walked out in time to hear my comment. "Well then, I need to be sure this first massage is everything you're looking for. Per your request, it will be a deep tissue massage, and I plan to add hot stones, too. How does that sound?"

"Heavenly. I can't wait."

As soon as I lay face down on the warm cushioned table, I could feel myself relax. Sophie applied fragrant massage oil and started on my shoulders, and we chatted as she worked on the knots. She was an eager sounding board for my wedding plans. The details had been swirling in my brain since I'd seen the barn, and it was good to share them with someone.

"Enough about me, Sophie. Tell me about you. What an interesting combination—an esthetician and massage therapist who's also a jewelry designer. How does that happen?"

There was a pause as she used her thumb on a particularly painful knot. "There, got it. You're doing great. The short story is it happened because of my parents. Mum was a receptionist at a hotel day spa, and Dad was a jeweler. I wanted to live at the spa with its peaceful, calming vibe, but Dad's craftsmanship fascinated me. When he found me at home fashioning bracelets with string and beads, he set up a workstation for me in his shop. I literally learned at his knee."

"And you pursued both fields. Obviously, you have certification as a massage therapist and an esthetician. Do you also have formal training in jewelry making?"

She laughed. "I'm not quite that ambitious. Dad taught me metalworking and soldering and how to set stones. The rest I learned by doing."

I was a wet noodle by the time she finished with me. When I met her at the reception desk, the first thing I did was book a second massage. "Let's set up a facial tomorrow and the massage the following day. And, when I'm alert, I want to look at your jewelry more closely."

Handing me a glass of water, she reminded me of the need to hydrate. "Sit for a second, Leta. No need to rush off."

Sophie was right. I had a leisurely day at my disposal and no reason to rush. Taking her advice, I made myself comfortable in the lobby. *If only a massage therapist would move to Astonbury,* I thought. *I'd be there at least every other week.*

I was leaving when she called my name. "Leta, you forgot your rings."

Thanking her profusely, I slipped my engagement ring on my left hand, and my garnet ring on the other. "It's all your fault, you know. I'm so relaxed, I can't think straight."

"You have amazing taste, Leta. The craftsmanship on these pieces is something to behold, and the filigree work on the diamond ring is exquisite."

Laughing, I explained that Dave's father deserved the credit for the engagement ring, since he gave it to Dave's mom. "I'll take the credit for the garnet, though. As soon as I saw it, I had to have it."

The rest of my day was unhurried and relaxed, a welcome change from my typical vacations to festivals or to see family. A week of pampering, leisurely strolls, and reading was long overdue, and today, the manor house was quiet. Lavinia had taken Belle and Ellie to Deddington for lunch and shopping, and Wendy was off with Edward. Rhiannon and I enjoyed a light lunch before she left for her appointment at the spa.

Dickens was fine with the lazy morning, but by midafternoon, he'd had enough. I was reading contentedly in an easy chair in my room when he put his head in my lap. "Horses and puppies, Leta. When do we see them?"

"I know. I promised. Let me finish this chapter, and we'll go. And I'll take your ball."

Edith had told us to help ourselves to carrots for the horses, so I grabbed a handful from the basket in the kitchen. As we passed the front desk, Bash called to me. "Good thing you've got a hood, Leta. The sun's out now, but the rain is coming. I'll have a towel ready for Dickens." We lived in England. Of course, rain was coming in.

Happy to be outside, Dickens pranced by my side. "Leta, you need to meet the cat. Rhubarb looks like Christie except he has a white mustache. I found him in the laundry room." Leave it to my boy to find not only the laundry room but also a cat. We'd only been here one night, and already he had two new friends plus puppies.

"Tell me you didn't play in the towels or sheets, Dickens." That was his favorite pastime at the Olde Mill Inn in Astonbury.

"It was much more fun than that. We explored the carriage house, and Rhubarb showed me his favorite room, the one with boxes of rags." I was only half listening. A room with rags? I imagined a house this old had plenty of ancient linens and curtains, and the carriage house was as good a place as any to store them.

Gemma stood chatting with Annabelle in the stable yard. "Leta, Annabelle tells me I'm welcome to ride every afternoon. I may never leave this place."

Smiling, I wandered into the stables with Dickens. He skidded to a stop at the entrance to the puppy stall, as I thought of it.

"Quiet," he yipped as he slowly lowered his haunches to the floor.

I knelt beside him, and we both watched in fascination as Lucky nursed her puppies. "They'll be sleepy after this, Dickens, so they won't want to play, but Lucky may. Let's feed the horses until she's done."

We were feeding our second horse when I heard Rob. "Luv, Annabelle's old enough to make her own decisions. I like James, but if our girl wants to venture out before she settles down, so be it. It won't do to nag her."

Edith emerged from a doorway and called over her shoulder. "I disagree. Someone needs to talk some sense into her."

When she spied me, she looked taken aback but recovered quickly. "Hi, Leta. If you need more carrots, Rob keeps plenty here in the office."

"Thanks, but Dickens would stay all day, if I let him, so we'll stop with this batch. He's hoping Lucky will want to play a bit when she's done nursing the pups. If not, you'll probably see us again later."

Lucky was napping when we checked, so I had to promise Dickens we'd return. We left in time to see Gemma walking to the manor house. "Wait up. Tell me about your ride."

"It was supposed to be an hour, but with no other guests, Annabelle was generous with her time. It was like being in another world. Nothing but birds singing and squirrels here and there. My entire day has been a delight."

"I had a massage and a relaxing day. I'm sure it's noisier with more guests, but the grounds are so extensive, you don't get traffic noise. Serene. That's the word." I tossed the ball for Dickens. "How was your massage?"

"Good enough that I scheduled another one. And did you see Sophie's work? Mum's not much on jewelry, but a carving set could be a hit. Emilia gave a set to Charlotte for Christmas with some kind of green stones that resemble emeralds."

She pulled a business card from her pocket. "Sophie Eliza Green. I feel like I've seen her name somewhere, but I can't think where. I wonder if she advertises her jewelry. Maybe that's it."

I stopped in my tracks. "Well, would you look at that." Edward was helping Wendy to dismount from her horse in front of the manor house. She braced her arm on his chest to steady herself, and like a scene from a movie, he lifted her hand to his lips and kissed it.

"Smooth," said Gemma. "Very smooth, but is he Prince Charming or a wolf in disguise?"

"My sentiments exactly." For once, we were in total agreement.

Wendy was nowhere in sight when we opened the front door, but Rhiannon was munching an apple by the front desk. "You two seem to have your feet firmly planted on the ground—unlike Wendy who just floated through here."

"Don't forget me," Dickens barked. "My feet are right here."

Shaking his head, Bash murmured, "Another one on cloud nine. Not sure how he does that." When I blinked in surprise, he blushed. "Sorry, shouldn't have said that."

Gemma encouraged him. "Oh, don't stop now. Tell us more. Does your uncle have a reputation?"

"To hear Mum and Dad talk, Uncle Edward was a bit of a playboy on the Continent. Before he married the countess, I assume. And from what I've seen since he became a widower, it's as if women swoon at his feet."

"He only had eyes for Wendy last night," said Rhiannon. "Is that what does it, the total focus? Admittedly, he's a handsome man, but there's got to be more to it."

"And," said Gemma, "Wendy has a boyfriend." She looked at me. "Has she gone off Rhys, or vice versa?"

"You'd think I'd be the first to know, but I don't." It was time I found out.

With Dickens by my side, I knocked on Wendy's door. She was in her robe with her phone to her ear when she answered the door. "Because it was late when I got in last night. Yes, I saw it, but I was busy. We'll see." She rolled her eyes. "Leta's here. Let me run."

She sat on the bed. "Suddenly, Rhys has time for me. He was worried when I didn't immediately return his call or respond to his text. Now he knows what it's like."

"Trouble in paradise?"

"I don't want to talk about it. I'm basking in the glow of someone focusing on me for a change."

When I flopped beside her, it did the trick. "Leta, it's fascinating. Edward hangs on my every word."

"And it's easy to see you're receptive."

"Only because it's a pleasant change." She cleared her throat. "I told him today that I was in a relationship."

"And?"

"He kissed me! He said, 'If you were happy, you would have told me that at the outset.' He's quite persistent, so much so that he's taking me to dinner tomorrow night."

"You just said it, Wendy. You're in a relationship. What are you thinking?"

She blushed. "I'm not sure I know. Let's just say that this interlude may clarify some things for me."

Talk about cryptic comments.

CHAPTER FIVE

UNTIL WENDY TOLD ME what was going on or invited my input, there wasn't much I could do. I sent Dave a few pics of Dickens with the horses, and he responded, "And now it's naptime." He knew me so well. I wanted the same thing for Wendy—a man who loved her the way Dave loved me. Rhys might not be that man, but it didn't mean Edward was.

I slept a bit too long and had to rush to get downstairs for dinner. Thankfully, there was no formal cocktail hour tonight. As Dickens and I exited the elevator, I heard voices coming from the study.

Gemma would call it snooping, but all I had to do was pause by the closed door. I couldn't make out every word, but I easily identified the voices as those of St. John and Edward.

"Not again, Edward." St. John's voice was tight, clipped. "When are you going to learn to live within your means?"

Edward let out a soft chuckle. "Soon, I promise. But I've got dinner plans, and, well, my credit cards are being terribly uncooperative."

A sharp exhale. "I thought you sold a painting. Did that fall through?"

"Just a slow payment." Edward's tone was unbothered. "And I have another commission in the works. I'm just a little short until next month."

I heard a rustling sound, and then a dull thud—money being thrown on the table? "Here," St. John said gruffly. "But this is the last time. Isn't it enough you've got a roof over your head? Not to mention food and drink?"

Hearing footsteps, I moved on and chattered to Dickens. "Come on. I'm ready for a glass of wine, but first we're taking a short walk."

The rain hadn't come in yet, but the wind was picking up, and it was all I could do to shut the door behind me. The gazebo was too far to walk, so Dickens and I chose the well-lit path to the carriage house. A warm glow came from the windows in the spa and from the second level. As I was wondering what was up there, what I took to be a cat dashed past me.

"That was Rhubarb," Dickens barked. "Must be chasing something. He's way faster than Christie."

"Are you dissing your sister, young man? You know she's much too prissy to chase things."

Dickens and I were the last ones to the table. I snagged the remaining chair, and Dickens slid beneath the table next to Belle. He knew who the softest touch was. Tonight, we were on our own for dinner, with the exception of Bash, who was our server.

"It's the norm for us to eat in the family wing," he said. "We've been successful at establishing Foxbourne Park as a destination resort rather than a B & B where the hosts are always around. In high season, when we're fully staffed, I have help with the front desk, and Edith has kitchen staff and servers. Mum is mostly behind the scenes, and Dad hasn't completely given up his other businesses. The spa, of course, is Emilia's baby."

Ellie and Belle carried the dinner conversation. They'd spent the afternoon visiting Deddington with Lavinia, and Belle admitted she was exhausted. "I'm looking forward to time at the spa tomorrow, and a quiet day in my room or by the fireplace down here."

I was excited about Belle's first visit to a spa. "Belle, you're going to love it. It will set the stage for relaxing the rest of the day."

That got a smile from Gemma. "Unless you're like me and decide to go horseback riding afterward." She turned to Wendy. "How was your riding experience today?"

"Very enjoyable, but I overdid it. I'm beginning to ache in muscles I didn't know I had. It will be an early night for me."

If I hadn't overheard Edward, I would have wondered why he wasn't on her dance card tonight, too. It was going to be an interesting week.

As Bash cleared the final courses, I asked if I could visit the kitchen. "I thought I'd see if there are any leftover bones available for Dickens."

"I'll tell Edith what you're looking for, and you can drop by whenever you like. She'll be in there several more hours prepping for breakfast. Why don't you pop in through the outside door when you and Dickens take your last walk? It's opposite the spa entrance and easy to spot."

Calling it a night, Wendy and Belle took the elevator upstairs as the rest of us retired to the drawing room, where a roaring fire greeted us. We were a quiet group as we settled into the comfy chairs, and it didn't take long before we too decided it was time for bed.

"Chop, chop, Dickens. One last walk, and then we're off to bed, too." He must have read my mind because he snuffled his way toward the spa as I shivered in the cold. Lights still glowed on the second level of the carriage house, but not inside the spa.

The lantern above the kitchen door made it easy to find, and the aromas that greeted me were enticing. Sniffing the air, I suspected Edith was serving something cinnamon for breakfast. In the short entryway, coats hung on pegs above a long bench with wellies beneath it. Shelves on the opposite wall held baskets filled with all kinds of paraphernalia, and a short flight of stairs led to the next level.

Voices drifted from the kitchen, and I paused on the top step. Edith sat at the large table, a pad of paper in front of her, pen in hand. I realized that the second voice came from the speaker on her phone.

"No thanks, Mum. I'm not at home."

Edith's hand stilled, the pen poised in midair.

"That's okay, Annabelle. I can put it in your fridge, and you can reheat it when you get in."

"Mum, I'm out to dinner. No need to bring food."

Edith's face lit up. "How nice that James has the night off."

There was no response, and Edith's grip tightened on the pen.

"You're not *with* James, are you?" Her voice wavered, her fingers curling tighter. "Annabelle ... it's him, isn't it?"

"Mum, I'm not having this conversation again."

"I just ... I can't believe you're still spending time with him—"

"Not now, Mum."

It was too late, when Edith yelled, "Don't you hang up on me!"

She dropped the pen and grabbed the phone, pulling it close to her ear. Her knuckles whitened as she muttered something under her breath and stabbed at it with her finger. When she slammed the phone down, her expression was thunderous. She stared at it, breathing hard.

That was when I called out. "Hello, Edith. It's Leta Parker and Dickens."

It took her a moment to recover her composure. "Sorry, didn't hear you come in. You've come for the bones, haven't you? Let me show you what I've picked out for your boy."

The awkward moment faded as Dickens trotted to her side, and she ruffled his fur. "Well, aren't you a handsome boy?"

Placing several bones on the floor in front of him, she let him choose. I grinned when he settled on the large knuckle bone. "That will keep him occupied. Do you by chance have a rag I can put down in my room? That way, there will be no danger of him staining anything."

She came up with a ragged towel, and I motioned Dickens to the dining room. "Thanks, Edith. We'll get out of your hair now."

Who was James, and who was Annabelle's dinner date? Something about the conversation unsettled me. I knew families had their secrets, but Edith's concern seemed deeper than the usual motherly worry.

If I'd been sharing a room with Wendy, we'd be discussing the conversation between Edith and her daughter and trying to figure out who was who. Instead, I surfed the internet for wedding dress ideas. Nothing I saw fit the image that was taking shape in my mind, so next I typed "Cotswolds seamstresses who make wedding dresses" into the search bar.

There were quite a few around Astonbury, and I knew I'd found the perfect one when I read the words, "Bespoke bridal wear—we work collaboratively with brides to create custom wedding dresses." I texted Dave goodnight before I snuggled beneath the comforter with visions of wedding dresses dancing in my head.

My facial appointment wasn't until ten, so I slept in before taking Dickens on a quick walk. Bash was at the front desk when we returned. "Are you ready for breakfast? If you hurry, you can catch Belle."

Alone in the dining room, Belle sipped her tea as Bash set a place for me.

"Good morning, Belle. How did you sleep?"

"I must admit I tossed and turned a bit. I'm anxious about having a massage. The idea of removing my clothes for anyone other than a doctor is unnerving."

This was a first. The Belle I knew never failed to be up for something new. I thought for a moment. "Belle, since we both have appointments at ten, why don't we arrive at 9:30, so you can get comfortable with the setup?"

She blushed. "That might help."

Leaving Dickens to man the desk with Bash, I took Belle through the kitchen. That way would be easier for her than the front steps.

Edith was loading the dishwasher and jumped as I opened the door. "My, you startled me. Come for more bones?"

"Thanks, but Dickens is fine for now. We're taking the short-cut to the spa."

With a distracted look, she turned back to the dishwasher and waved us through. I imagined her to-do list was a mile long, what with lunch and dinner prep.

A large tuxedo cat lolled outside in front of the door to the spa. *Is this Rhubarb?* When I opened the door, he or she sprang to life and darted in.

Before she welcomed us, Emilia shooed the cat back out. "Rhubarb! Out all night and wanting Sophie to feed you, no doubt." She took our jackets and offered a choice of herbal teas. As Belle studied the artwork, I quietly explained to Emilia why we were so early.

"No problem, Leta. Her concerns aren't unusual. I'll show her around and answer her unspoken questions. And Sophie will be down shortly. She prepared the room last night, after her six p.m. client, so the only thing to do is to turn on the heating pad and oil diffuser."

She poured hot water in the teacups. "In fact, I'll switch everything on, so Belle gets the full experience, even before Sophie arrives."

Handing Belle her tea and a brochure, Emilia started with a story about Lavinia. "Belle, I must tell you that Grandmother has fallen in love with Sophie and now gets weekly massages. She only begrudgingly allows us to bump her when we need her spot for a guest. Now, enjoy your tea, and I'll be right back."

I was pointing out Edward's signature on the rose garden painting when Emilia shrieked and stumbled from the treatment room. "I think . . . I think he's dead."

Running to her, I grasped her arms and looked over her shoulder. I knew immediately that she was right. I don't know how, but I did. "Belle, call Gemma," I said, as I moved Emilia to a chair and returned to the doorway.

All I could think was, *I don't want to do this, but delaying won't change anything.* The man was lying face down on the table as though waiting for a massage. What marred the peaceful pose was a dagger in his back—a bejeweled dagger. Oddly, I saw hardly any blood. The other thing that caught my eye was a small tattoo on his left shoulder blade, an artist's palette and paintbrush.

It confirmed for me what I'd suspected almost immediately. I couldn't see his face, but the blond curls on his neck, the muscular build? Who else could it be?

I stuck my head out of the door. "Belle, did you get Gemma?"

She assured me Gemma was on her way just as I heard Sophie's voice. "Why, hello, Belle. You must be eager to . . ."

Taking in the tableau, she stuttered to a stop. "Emilia, what's wrong?"

Emilia's mouth opened, but no words came out. It seemed an age before she blinked and motioned toward me.

"Sophie," I said, and hesitated. *How am I supposed to say this?* "Sophie, Edward is on your massage table, and . . . he's dead."

CHAPTER SIX

I was saved from having to say more when Gemma came in the door. Dressed in running gear, she was red-faced and breathing hard. She read the room and turned to me. "Leta, what's happened? Belle said it was urgent, but nothing more."

Whispering, I pulled her into the treatment room. "That's because I didn't tell her anything, but now they know. It's Edward Foxbourne, and he's dead. And before you ask, I didn't find him. It was Emilia."

She stuffed her gloves in her pockets before carefully stepping to the table and feeling for a pulse on Edward's neck. "He's cold. If I had to judge, I'd say he's been here most of the night."

Stepping back, she surveyed the room. "I know you haven't touched anything. You know better. Let me call 999."

I listened as she relayed the situation. "DI Taylor here, of the Stow-on-the-Wold station in Gloucestershire. I'm a guest at Foxbourne Park, and there's been a death. Yes, in the spa adjacent to the manor house. Yes, I'm on the scene, and you need to know it's a suspicious death."

She rolled her eyes, a typical Gemma reaction. "Because there's a dagger in the victim's back. Yes, I can secure the scene."

Ducking into the waiting area, she explained the police were on their way. "Emilia, have you already told Sophie and Belle what you saw?"

When all three of the women nodded, Gemma managed the situation as best she could. "I know this is an awful shock, but I need you to avoid discussing it any further until we've gathered more information."

She turned to Belle. "Can you make tea, please? With plenty of sugar." Sweet tea was the British cure for everything. I wasn't sure there was an American equivalent.

When she rejoined me, she held her hand out palm up. "Please proceed. I know you're dying to."

"No. Not this time. You know I want to write murder mysteries—not get mixed up in them."

"So you've said, but that didn't stop you from getting in Jake's way at that writers' conference. He said you were right in the middle of his case."

It was true that I'd been instrumental in solving that case, not that I'd intended to. "Are those Jake's words or your interpretation? As I recall, he invited me to keep my ear to the ground, despite my telling him I was there to work on writing."

"Whatever. Do I want you snooping around, asking questions? No, but I do value your attention to detail."

Those words meant that today, I had the appreciative Gemma. That wasn't often the case. Against my better judgment, I gave in and did what she asked.

Studying the body from the doorway, I observed something I hadn't initially noticed. "His arms are flung out in front of him, hanging off the table. Could that have been his only reaction to being stabbed? Does that mean death was instantaneous?"

"I'd say yes to both. There are no signs of a struggle. Our killer hit just the right spot, whether by accident or because they know something of anatomy. Plunging the dagger between the shoulder blades on the upper left—they likely hit the heart. I doubt this was luck."

My eyes returned to the dagger. "Why did it have to be one studded with garnets? I may never look at my ring or necklace in quite the same way again."

Focusing on the stool and small chest at the top end, I noticed a pot for heating stones. Next to it on the chest was the oil diffuser Sophie would fill with different aromatic oils. The day before, it had been lavender. A flash of color caught my eye.

I gave Gemma a questioning look and pointed. When she gave me a go-ahead nod, I approached the chest. "It's an earring—an emerald earring. I wonder if a client removed it and left it here by accident. But where's the other one?"

Gemma pulled out her notebook and jotted a note. She never went anywhere without it. "Good question. If it were my case, I'd speak with Sophie immediately after Emilia."

Turning clockwise, I surveyed the wide chest of drawers against the wall. I suspected the drawers held blankets and sheets, as Sophie would have to change the linens for each client. A gilt-framed mirror hung on the wall above it. Atop the chest were candles and the decorative tray where I'd placed my jewelry yesterday.

I turned toward the wall behind me and saw hooks holding Edward's clothes on the narrow wall to the left of the door. That left only the wall opposite the chest of drawers. Against it was an upholstered bench that held a bolster and two decorative pillows.

I studied the oversized painting above it. It was another Edward Fox piece, an abstract featuring hands and butterflies. That was the only way I knew to describe it. "Gemma, did you notice yesterday that all the artwork is by Edward Foxbourne—or Fox, as he signed them? I wonder if he's known in the art world."

Her phone chirped before she could respond. "DI Taylor." A look of surprise appeared on her face, followed by a slow smile. "Will? I can't believe it's you. You did, did you? That's right. A dagger in the back. Hold on."

Holding up her hand, she left the room, and I heard her open the outside door. Gemma wouldn't blithely tell someone about the dagger, so who was Will?

Her departure gave me time to circle the room again. Working my way counterclockwise toward the foot of the table, I slowly arrived back at Sophie's stool at the far end. I stared at the earring and wondered how someone had walked out with only one. Wouldn't they notice right away they were missing the mate?

What made me drop to my hands and knees, I couldn't say. I started to run my hands beneath the chest but knew Gemma would shoot me if I touched anything. Instead, I put my cheek to the floor and looked. Nothing, but when I turned my head toward the rolling stool, there it was. Hidden next to a wheel was the other earring. One mystery solved.

When Gemma opened the door, her pursed lips told me something was amiss. "That was my old boss, DCI Harper, from Thames Valley station in Oxford. Of course, the Deddington station alerted him that there was a death at Foxbourne Park. A viscount's estate? There was no question they'd contact him."

"Is he on his way, then? Or sending someone from Deddington?"

"Neither. He's drafting me into service. His exact words were, 'I hear tell your team handled the death of an earl on your home turf, so Viscount Foxbourne will be in good hands.' Will's in London as part of a counter-terrorism task force and can't get here until late evening."

"But surely he's sending someone to secure the scene. You don't have Constable James here to help. And what about interviewing everyone? Isn't it important to do that sooner rather than later?"

That got me an eye roll. "Yes, Tuppence, it is, but before I get to that, I need to notify the family. The local constable and the Scene of Crime Officers are at an accident scene the other side of Deddington—involving a herd of sheep, if you can believe it—so it will be some time before they get here. The only saving grace is that the Family Liaison Officer will be here any minute."

She blew out her lips. "Remember how we handled notifying the victim's family at Astonbury Manor when Ellie found the body?"

How could I forget? When Constable James was delayed in getting there, she'd asked me to observe reactions and unobtrusively take notes as she informed Ellie's guests that a member of their family was dead. When she was willing, Gemma and I worked well together.

"We'll work this the same way. You stay here for now. It's a good opportunity to look around the waiting area to see if anything looks out of place. I'll wait at the front steps for the FLO, and once I bring her up to speed, I'll call the family together. I'll text you when we're good to go."

My first thought was that I should stick to my commitment not to get involved. My second thought was about Wendy. "Oh my gosh! I know Wendy's only just met the man, but she—"

"I haven't forgotten her, nor Rhiannon and Ellie. Could be we pull them together immediately after the family and before we come back here. Ellie may wind up sitting with Lavinia, given that they're friends. I know it's sexist, but I see Ellie being more of a comfort than St. John."

So much for my wanting to remain on the sidelines. I tried to tell myself that taking notes for Gemma wasn't the same as being actively involved, but I knew better.

She bit her lip. "We've got our work cut out for us. Sooner rather than later, I also need to notify the Thompsons—Edith, Rob, and Annabelle."

At this rate, I'd be on duty all day. I could only hope the Deddington constable got here soon. In the waiting area, Sophie and Emilia were slumped in their chairs.

Thankfully, Belle shushed them as they sat up straight and began to ask me questions. "Girls, Leta can't tell you anything beyond what Gemma has already said."

Sophie rubbed her eyes. "I told him . . . wait until today."

Handing her a tissue, Emilia shook her head. "It's not the first time, Sophie. It's not your fault."

I couldn't let this pass. "What do you mean, Sophie? What needed to wait until today?"

"He was sore from his ride, but it was late . . . I missed his text." She put her face in her hands.

With her arm around Sophie, Emilia lifted her tear-stained face to me. "It was our agreement with him."

At my quizzical look, she explained. "He had an old shoulder injury from being thrown from a horse, and regular massages helped."

Sophie looked up. "When I could, I worked him in."

Was that why he was on the massage table? Because he was expecting a massage, not because he'd already had one? The disjointed story was confusing, and I'd have to give Gemma the heads-up to pursue the details.

CHAPTER SEVEN

IN THE FRONT HALL, Dickens knew something was off as soon as he saw us, but my finger to my lips told him not to ask. Before escorting the FLO to the kitchen, Gemma tasked Bash with gathering his father, mother, and grandmother in the drawing room. The only explanation she offered was that she had something important to tell them.

She was frowning when she joined Dickens and me in the dining room. "Not the way I wanted to do it, but I realized I had to tell Edith what was going on. Given how close she is to the family, I was relieved that she didn't fall apart at the news. She turned white as a sheet and stumbled to a chair, but it wasn't long before she said, 'They'll need tea,' and swung into action."

"Does she know not to discuss it with her family?"

"Yes. I explained I needed to speak with them before she did. I can only hope she'll follow my instructions."

From there, the plan played out as Gemma envisioned it. The Foxbourne family, except for Emilia, had assembled in the drawing room, and I took a seat by the window where I could see everyone's faces.

It was déjà vu when Gemma used nearly the same words she'd used at Astonbury Manor. "Thank you for your patience. I'm speaking to you now, not as a guest but in my capacity as a detective inspector, and I have some disturbing news. I'm sorry to tell you that Edward was found dead this morning."

The reactions weren't atypical. Lavinia blanched and Charlotte gasped. St. John's mouth dropped open, but he recovered quickly enough to see to his wife and mother. Seated between the two women, he grasped Charlotte's hand and then put his arm around Lavinia's shoulders.

It was St. John who spoke first. "Gemma, can you tell us when and where he was found? Was he out riding? That's usually where he is in the mornings."

"No, he wasn't outside. Emilia found Edward in the spa. She's understandably shaken. I've spoken with her only briefly, and I'll be conducting a more thorough interview with her shortly."

Charlotte stood. "Oh no, not Emilia. She must be in a terrible state."

"Emilia's doing as well as can be expected. Belle is with her in the spa." She took a breath. "She's a comforting presence."

As Charlotte reluctantly took her seat, Gemma proceeded more formally. "Unfortunately, given the circumstances, we're treating this as a suspicious death. We will be conducting a full investigation to determine exactly what happened."

Charlotte interrupted her. "You mean, it wasn't natural causes?"

Shaking her head, Gemma didn't miss a beat. "No. It wasn't. That's why we need to conduct a thorough investigation to determine exactly what happened."

"Where is Sophie? Was she there when Emilia . . . ?" Bash couldn't quite get the words out.

"She's in the spa, but she arrived just after Emilia found your uncle. They're both in good hands with Belle."

Gemma motioned to the FLO who had quietly entered the room. "I know this is an emotional time, and Detective Constable Atkins, our Family Liaison Officer, is here to help you with any support you may need. After I've interviewed Emilia and Sophie, I'll want to interview each of you to learn when and where you last saw Edward."

Though he was visibly shaken, St. John asked the logical question. "Gemma, may I ask why the Thames Valley Force isn't handling this? I appreciate your being here and expediting things, but where is our local constabulary?"

"Good question. I spoke with DCI Harper this morning. We used to work together, and he's asked me to step in during these critical early hours until he can get here from London."

Fortunately, St. John was a reasonable man and took in stride the news about DCI Harper's involvement with the counter-terrorism task force. "Thank you, Gemma. I know I speak for us all when I say we're in shock. I'd especially like to get our family physician here to tend to Mother and to check on Emilia, too. Beyond that, what can I do to help?"

She assured him that calling in the doctor was fine and asked if there was a room where she could conduct interviews. When he suggested the library in the family wing, she agreed and dismissed the group. "My only request is that you stay here at the manor house until I've had a chance to sit down with you."

Charlotte and St. John stood on either side of Lavinia to help her to her feet. Seeing how Lavinia struggled made me think of Ellie. Two years ago, she had lost her husband, her stepson, and a grandson in a few months' time, and I felt sure that experience would help her in comforting her friend.

I suggested that to Gemma, and she put her hand to her chin. "You're right, Leta. It's critical for me to get back to Emilia and Sophie, but I also need to inform Ellie, Rhiannon, and Wendy. If only the Deddington constable would get here."

As she stared out the window, I pictured options tumbling through her head. My proposal probably wouldn't fly, but I had to ask. "Gemma, shall I tell them? You'll want to interview them later, but I can at least let them know what's happened. They're together in the barn doing yoga."

She turned to me with a deep sigh. "Yes. I can't see any other way. They're sure to ask Bash when they come in the front door, and he's distraught enough already without having to deal with that."

Until help arrived, she was stuck with me. "What else can I do to help, Gemma? Take notes while you interview Emilia and Sophie? What?" As I uttered these words, I knew I was dangerously close to crossing the line from merely observing to actively ferreting out information.

"All of the above. I'll check on Edith and then do another scan of the scene until you can get back to the spa."

In the barn, Rhiannon was conducting a combo class—chair yoga for Ellie and free standing for Wendy. She paused before shifting her students to another pose. "Class is nearly over, Leta, but feel free to join us for the restorative poses."

Wendy's legs up the wall pose looked inviting, but I knew it was too little too late for me. Instead, I took a seat. Maybe I could convince Rhiannon to do an evening session. By then, we'd all need it.

I hated to ruin the calm after she ended with namaste, but it had to be done. "Ladies, I've got some bad news."

Concerned about how Wendy would take the news, I waited until she resumed a cross-legged pose before I spoke. "Edward was found dead in the spa."

Her words came out in a whisper as she leaned toward me. "Edward?"

As she murmured almost to herself, I picked out only a few words. "Only yesterday . . . full of life. . ." She was probably imagining he'd had a heart attack, not that someone had killed him.

Dickens trotted to Wendy when I pointed to her. Still murmuring, she rubbed his nose as he put his head in her lap and licked her hands.

In a flowing movement, Rhiannon unfolded herself and stood. "Leta, that's awful. He seemed the picture of health."

I couldn't tell them yet about the dagger, but I could do better than Gemma's official language. "Belle and I were there when Emilia found him, and it was clear his death wasn't due to a health problem. I know if I say suspicious circumstances, you can translate."

Those words shook Wendy out of her fog. "You mean . . . you mean it was murder?"

Before I could do more than nod, Ellie grabbed her jacket. "Lavinia must be devastated. I'll go check on her. St. John and Charlotte will be glad for my help."

Her legs still folded beneath her, Wendy rocked back and forth. "He was charming, a harmless flirt. Who would want him dead?"

I knelt by her side. "Wendy, will you be okay? It's a shock for everyone, but you spent a lot of time with him over the last twenty-four hours."

She whispered that she'd be fine, though I wasn't convinced. Still, I took the bull by the horns. "I'm taking notes while Gemma interviews Emilia and Sophie, so I've got to run, but think about this. She'll interview us about our interactions with Edward, what we saw, what we heard. You spent more time with him than any of us, so you may be first. Do you think you can spend the next little while thinking back over everything you gleaned about him? You know your insights could be a tremendous help."

My words accomplished exactly what I'd hoped. Wendy sat up straight and shook her head as though clearing her brain. "You're right. And I want to do anything I can to help."

Turning to Rhiannon, I suggested the same to her. "You spent time with him at the bar that first night and sat at the dinner table with us. Even beyond what we got directly from Edward, we've picked up on little bits of background, like Bash mentioning his marriage."

And I knew he was an artist. "Wendy, did he mention his artwork to you? That's part of who he was."

A glimmer of a smile appeared on her face. "Yes. He wanted to do a charcoal sketch of me."

I couldn't help myself. I could hear him saying, "Come up and see my etchings." *He may have been charming, but was he harmless?*

CHAPTER EIGHT

BELLE WAS LEAVING THE spa when I arrived. "Gemma's concerned about Edith. She says she was a rock when she first told her about Edward, but she's going downhill fast. Constable Atkins has her hands full with the family, so I'm a family liaison officer again. I may have to come out of retirement and apply for the position officially."

With her comforting demeanor and nursing background, she was a natural. Gemma's boyfriend, Jake, had used Belle in the same capacity during a recent murder investigation. The bonus was that, as she put it, "it was amazing what people will tell a little old lady." She never failed to come away with uninvited confidences that shed light on the investigation.

She called over her shoulder as she crossed to the kitchen door. "By the way, be sure to ask Sophie about the jewelry display."

In the waiting area, I glanced at the display, but Gemma hopped to her feet before I could get a good look. "Thank goodness you're here."

She pulled me down the hall to a miniscule break room. "We'll do the interviews in here. The shock is taking its toll, and Emilia's fading fast. I need to finish with her and let her leave."

"From the looks of Sophie, she's not in much better shape. A comforting dose of four-legged companionship couldn't hurt. I'll fetch Emilia and ask Sophie to look after Dickens."

Giving Emilia the one comfortable chair, Gemma and I pulled two stools from beneath the counter. The offer of tea elicited a small smile from Emilia. "Heavens no. I'm drowning in tea."

Gemma was gentle with her. "I know this isn't easy, but I'd like you to take me through your arrival this morning, from the moment you unlocked the door until you found your uncle. Take your time."

A long, deep breath preceded her response. "It's a routine I follow without conscious thought. Punch in the code to unlock the door, flip the light switch on as I walk in. Come straight back here, drop my bag in a drawer, and hang up my coat." She pointed to a green jacket on a hook. "Then, I fill the electric kettle. Belle's been doing a lot of that this morning."

She closed her eyes. "Make my first cuppa and sit down at the front desk to review the schedule. Leta and Belle had ten a.m. appointments for today. Rhiannon and Wendy were down for after lunch, and a few locals were coming in later."

Her morning routine included checking the website for appointments and fiddling with social media. "Because the estate is closed until April, we're not that busy right now. It's just us and the stables that have any customers, and not that many."

Gemma guided her back to this morning. "What else did you do before Leta and Belle arrived?"

"Not much. I worked at the desk and fixed a second cup of tea. Just before they knocked on the door, I turned on the steamer for Leta's facial."

"Was there a reason you didn't turn on the equipment in the massage room?"

"There was no need. I knew Sophie would be down shortly to switch on whatever she planned to use for the first appointment. It might be hot stones. Sometimes she sets out an eye pillow. And she chooses her oil for the diffuser."

Again, a hint of a smile played across her face. "We both like to clean and straighten our rooms before we leave in the evenings, so we're not rushed when the day begins."

There was no avoiding the next question. "Emilia, what did you see when you opened the door?"

She sat up straight, as though bracing herself. "I saw Uncle Edward on the table. I saw . . . the dagger in his back."

"How did you know it was your uncle? Did you approach the table?"

"No! I knew right away because he's the only one who makes himself at home like that."

Gemma frowned. "What does that mean?"

"He. . . We . . . gave him free massages. Well, not exactly free. He offered us several of his paintings, so I guess you could say it was an exchange."

Glancing at me, Emilia explained about his shoulder injury and how massages helped. "The paintings you admired yesterday, Leta? I paid for a few of them. They were older works, and Uncle Edward didn't charge me much, but I didn't have the funds for as many as I needed. That's when he offered to let us work off the payment in massage treatments. Sophie was good about it. After all, I only do facial treatments."

"And what? He just showed up whenever he wanted?"

"No. He was supposed to text Sophie." She tilted her head. "I might have thought he was here for an early morning massage, except all the lights were off."

When I held up my hand, a look of irritation flashed across Gemma's face before she nodded. "Earlier, Sophie said something about a missed text. We'll need to ask her."

She finished by asking Emilia what else she noticed and whether she touched anything. Emilia had walked in and out so quickly, I was pretty sure she hadn't seen a thing.

The color drained from her face. "Just the dagger."

"Emilia, I know it was a shocking sight to see it in his back, but please think back. What else, if anything, did you notice about it?"

She bit her lip before blurting, "It was Sophie's. I mean, not hers personally, but she makes them, and we sell them."

"It's okay, Emilia. I understand what you mean." Gemma wrapped up by cautioning her not to share the details about Edward's death with anyone else. "We need to keep a tight lid on the information as we investigate. I'll reveal the circumstances to your father soon enough, but now is not the time."

Handing Emilia her coat and bag, I walked her to the waiting area. "If you want to talk, feel free to find me. Since I'm in the know, I'm the one person you can talk to other than Gemma, and I'm happy to lend an ear."

Dickens lay in front of Sophie in the waiting area with one paw stretched across her feet. She seemed calmer, and I was sure Dickens's presence had something to do with the change.

When we arrived in the break room, Dickens glanced from me to Sophie before sitting next to her chair. She mouthed "thank you," and placed her hand atop his head.

I couldn't quite put my finger on it, but Gemma's tone with Sophie was different. She started by inquiring about the last time Sophie had seen Edward. It didn't surprise me to hear it was Sunday night when she was serving dinner. If I hadn't learned about the massage-for-paintings arrangement, I would have thought they had very little contact.

From there, the interview grew more pointed. "So, how did he come to be on your massage table?"

"I knew he wanted a massage, but he's never just shown up like that."

"How did you know he wanted a massage?"

"He texted me around four Monday afternoon and wanted to come then, but I had a client. I suggested five thirty. He said that was too late, that he had dinner plans, and we went back and forth about after dinner. He can . . . could be quite insistent."

Gemma's eyes narrowed slightly. "And did he get that massage?"

"No, he didn't. We agreed on a time, but then after dinner, we went back and forth with him wanting to come later and later."

"And that was it? No massage?"

I could see Sophie was turning the question over in her mind. "No . . . I mean, he didn't give up, but he didn't get a massage."

Gemma leaned in slightly. "Lay it out for me, Sophie. What happened?"

"We originally agreed on eight," she said. "But he kept pushing it out. I told him nine was too late, but he was insistent."

Pulling her phone from her pocket, Sophie scrolled through her messages. "Here. You can see for yourself."

Gemma scanned the texts, her brow furrowing slightly as she read them aloud:

Edward – 8:00

Running late. Be there 8:30

Sophie – 8:01

Okay

Edward – 8:15 pm

Make it 9

Sophie – 8:16

No. Too late. Check with me tomorrow

Edward – 8:17

No way. See you at 9

Edward – 9:15

I'm here

Edward – 9:30

I'm here!

She did a double-take and handed me the phone, pointing to a photo. It was two emerald earrings. When my eyes opened wide, Gemma gave Sophie a stern look. "Please explain this photo."

"Oh, for goodness' sake. He'd been hounding me about a new design for those earrings. Something simpler, he said."

"Why didn't you respond to his last two texts?"

"Because I put my phone on Do Not Disturb so I could focus on the necklace and bracelet sets I was working on. I missed those texts when they came in."

Gemma's gaze remained intent. "And you didn't see them until when?"

"Around midnight when I took a break before starting on another set."

"And did you come downstairs when you saw them? Did you check to see if Edward was still here?"

Sophie shifted in her seat. "No. I figured he left when I didn't respond."

"That's odd, considering how persistent he was." She looked into the distance, then asked almost casually, "Did you check the spa at all?"

"No. I worked nearly all night on that order. I needed to ship it out today, and I was sure I'd hear from Edward in the morning."

Silence stretched between them before Gemma finally spoke. "Sophie, I need to ask you about the dagger."

There was a look of utter confusion on Sophie's face. "Dagger?"

"Yes," said Gemma, leaning toward Sophie. "The weapon used in Edward's death was a jeweled dagger, like the ones you make and sell here at the spa."

Sophie's face went pale. "I didn't know. All I heard was that Emilia found him on the massage table. Dead."

"I know your carving sets and daggers are on display here, in a locked case. Who had access to them besides you and Emilia?"

Sophie stammered. "Yes, they're in the glass case with the jewelry, but we're fairly lackadaisical about the lock. Someone would have to come behind the counter to open the case, and I can't imagine who would do that."

"I understand this is a shock. But I need you to think carefully. Did anyone show unusual interest in those carving sets or daggers? Did you notice anything missing or out of place recently?"

"No and no. Clients comment on both, but it's the jewelry they most often want to handle. The carving sets and daggers are much more expensive, and I don't sell as many. And I'd know if anything was missing. There've been three carving sets and three daggers in the case since December. Are they there now?"

Gemma didn't answer her. "What about sales, Sophie? How many have you sold?"

"During the busy season, I'd say two sets a month, more in November and December. Guests usually pick them up as gifts. Charlotte has a set on display in the dining room, and that helps. And Annabelle bought a set to give her parents for Christmas. Even a few locals have purchased them. Occasionally, women who are without their boyfriends or spouses will purchase a dagger as a gift. They don't sell as well as the sets."

I couldn't read the look on Gemma's face. Had she already checked the display case? Did she know whether a dagger was missing? Regardless, if the display was complete, there was no telling whose dagger had wound up in Edward's back.

In a calm voice, Gemma wrapped up the interview. "Sophie, we'll need to talk more about the dagger. But for now, I want you to stay available, and if you think of anything, no matter how small, you come to me."

"I will. I promise."

I'd been writing as fast as I could. It was tempting to ponder the new information as I jotted notes, but there was no time for that. Questions were swirling in my head.

Now, as Gemma escorted Sophie out, I made a list in no particular order. Downstairs? Emerald earrings? Display case? Now what? I underlined that last line.

What I really wanted to know was how much longer Gemma would need my help. I was in the middle of this mess now, and I'd hate to be summarily dismissed. No matter that I kept saying I was done with murder investigations, I'd be lying if I said I wasn't hooked.

Gemma interrupted my musings in a peremptory tone. "Nancy Drew, we've got work to do."

That must mean she wasn't dumping me yet. I half laughed at the rhyme but knew better than to mention it to her. "Okay. What's next on the agenda?"

She sat me down behind the front counter. "Don't touch. Tell me what you see on the glass shelves."

She doesn't want to hear about the jewelry. "Three jeweled carving sets—one in hematite, one in amethyst, and one in garnet—and two daggers. A dagger is missing!"

"Right you are. Two daggers, not three. Notice anything about the case itself?"

"The sliding door on the left is open a fraction. I wonder where the key is. Do you know?"

In response, Gemma pulled open the slim middle drawer above the kneehole of the desk. "Where everyone puts their keys—in the paperclip bowl. When Sophie said they were lackadaisical about the lock, she wasn't kidding."

I looked up at her. "So, this tells us that anyone who walked in here had the means. Was it opportunistic or premeditated? Did that someone grab whatever was at hand, or plan ahead because they knew it was readily available?"

"You know, you watch too many murder mysteries, don't you? Are you going to tell me the motive next, Sherlock? And, let's not forget opportunity. Who can get in here when Sophie and Emilia lock up and leave? Edward obviously could. We've got our work cut out for us. Right this minute, I need your eyes on the crime scene again. Your attention to detail is your superpower."

"I beg to differ. I think it's my 'uncanny ability' to get people to talk to me, as your boyfriend would say. Jake suggested hiring me to give his officers tips."

"Oh, for goodness' sake. How like him to encourage your nosey parker tendencies. Enough. Follow me."

When she closed the door behind us, I stopped her. "Gemma, before I forget, I found the other earring."

I pointed to the stool. "On the floor over there. Listen, do you want me to take pictures of things like that—the earrings and the clothes on the hooks? I refuse to take pictures of the body, but the rest, I can manage."

With her cheek on the floor, she took a look. "May as well. It will help to have the scene at our fingertips until the SOCOs document and share it."

"So, tell me, do you know something about these earrings that I don't? I expected you to ask Sophie more about them. As in new design for whom? Was Edward giving them to someone?"

My eyes widened as I heard Bash's words in my head. "Hold on. Do you remember Bash mentioning Edward had been married—to a countess, no less? Could they have belonged to his wife?"

Gemma blew her lips out. "Would you believe I have a method? I'll find out about the earrings, but the most important thing at this early stage is to establish a few facts about the dagger. I have plenty of follow-up questions for Sophie."

We worked well together. Because I'd given the scene the once-over earlier, it was her turn. She recited what she saw, and I took notes, adding details here and there. Before she moved on, I snapped pics.

When she stood over the body, she commented that it would take strength to drive the dagger in. "Leta, what do you make of the tattoo?"

"That it makes sense, given Edward is . . . was an artist." I glanced at the painting above the bench. "I have this idea that he didn't have much money, so I wonder why he was willing to take massages for his paintings in lieu of cash. Why do I think there was something more to that arrangement?"

"I have a sense there is, but I can't tell you why. Could it be because we've seen him work his charms on Wendy?"

A knock on the door interrupted that thought, and a woman about my age stuck her head inside. She introduced herself as the Chief Scene of Crime Officer. "May I come in?"

She was clad in white coveralls and booties. "You won't want to hear this, but Constable Lucas is delayed. The poor man who hit the sheep had a heart attack as we were processing the scene. The paramedics are transporting him to John Radcliffe in Oxford, and the constable is following with the wife. She was uninjured, but the situation further complicates everything. And you've probably heard there's a bloody snowstorm headed our way."

Gemma grimaced. "Seriously? That means DCI Harper will be stuck in London, and I'll be stuck in charge. Just shoot me now."

The Chief SOCO smiled. "I won't do that, but I will process this scene pronto and get the body out of here. The last thing you need is a body on the premises, eh?"

CHAPTER NINE

With the Chief SOCO in the treatment room, Gemma and I retreated to the waiting area, where she spoke with the other two SOCOs. "As you're dusting for prints, I see the most critical areas as the desk, the counter, and that glass display case. Perhaps the carving sets and daggers. And I know it's probably useless, but please dust the door to the treatment room and the front door too."

"Gemma," I said, "you mentioned access earlier, but I think I may have the answer." I flipped through my notes. "Emilia said she punched in the code to unlock the door. There must be a keypad outside. Someone other than Emilia and Sophie must know the code. Maybe Edward, but who else?"

She tilted her head. "Good catch. Can you run upstairs and ask Sophie the code? And see what she has to say about who else might have it?"

Holding up my hand, I flipped back to the interview questions. "You asked Sophie if she came downstairs to check on Edward. What's upstairs? Why would she be up there?"

"What? I know something you don't? Alert the media." I could see she was trying not to smile. "She lives up there and has a small area for a studio. She mentioned it during my massage yesterday."

She directed me down the hall, where I found a door beyond the break room. It opened to a tiny foyer with a set of stone stairs on the left and a door to the outside directly ahead. A long, narrow hall at the top appeared to span half the width of the carriage house. I knocked on the door with the decorative iron G hanging on it.

I wouldn't say Sophie was happy to see me, but she was gracious. "Come in, Leta. I'm making cocoa. Would you like some?"

To the left of the door was a small kitchen with a counter and two stools, but Sophie motioned me to an arrangement of overstuffed chairs in the center of her flat. It faced an expanse of windows looking out on the manor house.

"What an inviting sitting area, Sophie. Perfect for reading a good book."

"I'm sure it is," she said, "but I spend most of my time in my studio." She gestured to a partially closed door on the right and frowned. "Are you here to check my stock? I can assure you that once I complete a carving set, I move it downstairs, or on occasion, ship it directly to a customer. I have a few up here that are in the early stages before I add the stones, but that's it."

I had only one simple question, but since I had her talking, this could be an opportunity to glean more information. "No, Sophie, I'm not here for that. I need the code for the front door, but I'd love to see your studio if you're in the mood for a tour."

"It's 1608, the year the first Sir Reginald started construction on the manor house."

"Ah, I remember something about 1688, but not that earlier date. Is it just you and Emilia who know it?"

She gave me a funny look. "I expect you figured out that Edward had the code. He was forever changing out artwork and wanted to be able to come and go when it suited him. If he could sell a painting he'd already sold us on the installment plan, he would replace it with another."

"But no one else?"

"Only St. John. Except he has his own code. He insisted on having one for safety purposes in case we took it into our heads to change ours. He didn't want to have to bust the door down if we were hurt or set the place on fire with our equipment. He's so funny. For whatever reason, he worries about our pots of hot wax and stones."

"Aww, that's kind of sweet."

As we sipped our cocoa, the tuxedo cat I'd seen earlier wandered in and leaped into her lap. "This is Rhubarb," Sophie said. "He's much happier here than he was in London. I couldn't let him roam there."

"Cats are a wonder, aren't they? When I first moved to my cottage, I kept Christie inside until I thought she was acclimated enough not to take off. Now, she's content to sun herself in the garden or on top of the stone wall and, knock on wood, never wanders."

That led to more talk of the oddities of cat behavior. "Rhubarb wanders far and wide, and he even follows me to the stables when I take riding lessons."

"From Annabelle?"

"Yes. Can you believe I'd never been close to a horse until I moved here? Edith encouraged me to visit the horses with carrots, but it was Annabelle who convinced me to get up on one."

A look of wonder crossed her face. "It was scary, but I enjoyed it. And Annabelle's been giving me lessons, if you can call it that. Mostly, we walk the trails on horseback."

For a moment, Sophie was the happy girl I'd met yesterday. Hoping she would ask me to stay, I set my mug down. "I'll get out of your hair now, unless you're up for showing me your studio."

My suggestion worked. "Why not? Maybe it will put me in the mood to work on a few things."

The studio was smaller than her sitting area with fewer windows, but still light and airy. She opened the double doors of a cabinet that held neatly labeled trays of semi-precious stones, wires, and colorful silk cords. The workbenches held an array of tools, only a few of which I could identify.

As we circled the room, Sophie used words that were new to me—diamond tip burr, flex shaft, and mandrels, among others. A jeweler's torch rested on its stand, ready for melting recycled silver into sleek, polished handles for the carving sets. She pointed out a small rolling mill against the wall, and explained she used it to shape the metal into rods or sheets. Nearby, a set of tiny files and fine-grit sandpaper waited for the final touch, smoothing the silver before it was inlaid with semi-precious stones.

"This is amazing, Sophie. How long have you been doing this?"

Her face brightened. "Since Dad took away my string and beads."

Was this the explanation I was looking for? Did she know how to reset fine jewelry?

"You're taking me back, Leta. Dad died several years ago, but he owned a London jewelry shop for forty years. He was known for his simple yet elegant designs. I've taken a different path, working with silver, iron, and semi-precious stones instead of gold. The formal education and certifications never felt right for me—I've always preferred to learn by doing, picking things up as I go along."

She explained how she often drew out her designs, but was just as likely to start working with the materials to see where an idea would take her. That's how seeing a jeweled dagger in a museum had led eventually to her daggers and carving sets. Initially, she set the stones in prongs, until she realized that a smooth bezel setting would make the handles more comfortable to hold.

"Sophie, would you use these same tools to set precious stones?"

"Oh yes. In fact, a few of these belonged to my father. I've reset some of my own jewelry, but I don't do it professionally. Wait one sec, and I'll show you what I mean."

She went through the sitting room to what must have been the bedroom door. When she returned, she carried a long gold chain with a large amethyst pendant.

"This stone was once part of a choker Dad made for my mum. When Mum died, I tried to wear it a few times, but it was much too elaborate for my tastes. It was only after Dad was gone that I felt like I could rework it. Now, I wear the pendant all the time and even have several loose stones remaining. I've been considering a ring but haven't settled on a design."

She handed me the necklace and pointed to my garnet ring. "I have two amethysts about that size—not square cut but oval like my pendant. After seeing your ring, I think I may work on a similar design with one stone."

Now was my chance. "Tell me about the emerald earrings."

Avoiding my gaze, she hesitated. "Just a favor Edward wanted."

I rolled my eyes. "Humor me, Sophie. He was making a play for Wendy, and those earrings make me think he already had a girlfriend. Were they a gift for another woman?"

When those words popped out of my mouth, I second-guessed myself. "Except why would he want a new design? Did he get them at a pawnbroker's or something?"

Sophie latched onto those words. "It could be. I didn't see much of Edward except for when he came and went here at the spa, and it wasn't as though we discussed his love life."

Looking at the amethyst necklace, I wondered aloud. "If he was interested in a special gift, you were certainly the gal to ask. I like the simplicity of your designs, and he must have too. Did he have a particular design in mind?"

Suddenly she covered her mouth and coughed. "We hadn't gotten that far."

She was being evasive, and I couldn't put my finger on why. Maybe Gemma would get more when she interviewed her again. I was happy to ask a question or two to push the investigation along, but that was as far as I wanted my involvement to go.

It was a good thing I had the code, because the door to the spa was locked. I saw the SOCOs removing Edward's body as I walked down the hall. One thing was for sure. Unless there was another treatment room on offer, further massages were out of the picture for me.

I gave Gemma the code and let her know St. John had a second one. "I don't have a keypad at my cottage, but my sister uses them at her homes in Georgia. Emilia should be able to tell you who came and went, right? And when."

She stared at her notebook with a distracted look on her face. "It's time I notified Rob and Annabelle at the stables, and I think it's best to take Edith with me. I wonder if she's already served lunch to the Foxbournes."

"How can I help? Do you want me at the stables taking notes?"

Stuffing her notebook in her parka, she looked up. "What if you and Belle man the kitchen? Based on the updates I'm getting from the FLO, I think she has her hands full with the family."

"I'm on it. Any word on the constable?"

That got a grimace. "Nothing good. The snow hasn't reached us yet, but it's started in Slough, and it's on the way. If he doesn't make it soon, he won't."

As I left the spa, I caught sight of Bash going around the corner of the carriage house carrying a paper sack and thought he must be taking Sophie lunch. I'd check later to be sure. If not, it would be an excuse for me to make another visit and see if I could glean any additional information from her.

That errant thought stopped me in my tracks. I had made a promise to myself to write mysteries, not solve them. Just because I'd set writing aside for a bit didn't mean detective work was on the table again. I pictured a cartoon bubble over my head with the words, "I will not get involved."

It was clear Belle had already taken charge in the kitchen. She was stirring a large pot of soup, and Rhiannon and Wendy were on sandwich duty.

Dickens looked up at me. "It's lunchtime."

Edith stood staring into the refrigerator but turned as I came in. Her pallor and red-rimmed eyes told me Edward's death was taking its toll. "We'll soon be serving lunch, and I think we're well stocked for the storm. Gemma's asked that I head home, and Belle's offered to take over for the afternoon."

"And Edith, we can all pitch in. We can handle dinner too, if you feel comfortable with that arrangement. If you've got feta cheese and kalamata olives on hand, I can make a mean Greek salad. Regardless, I can throw something together, and we can all follow recipes."

She wiped her hands on her apron and dropped into a chair. "You ladies are too kind. I don't want to leave the Foxbournes in the lurch, but I need to be there for my family. Annabelle and Rob will take this hard."

I put my hand on her shoulder. "And you, Edith, how are you doing? You grew up with Edward. This has to be a blow."

Tears shone in her eyes. "It is. When he comes home, he's never here for long, but I can't believe he's gone. That he won't be back."

Taking a seat beside her, I rubbed her back. "It sounds like he was here for a month or two this time. That must make it even harder."

It was as though I'd taken a stopper from a bottle. Tears and memories flowed unchecked. "Aye. And this time, he was on his own. When he finally married a few years back, he would occasionally bring his wife, but before that, it was always a different woman. Still, he always managed to sneak into the kitchen and make himself at home."

She swiped at her tears. "If he wasn't stealing biscuits, he was off riding or up in the studio with his latest model." She pointed to a small canvas on the far wall. "Did that on one trip."

It was a 12 x 12 painting of a woman in an apron, looking up from the stove. I walked over to get a better look. She was smiling, and a tendril of red hair had escaped her white scarf. "Edith, this is you. He captured you perfectly."

The corners of her mouth turned up a tiny bit. "He must have sketched it one day while I was working and painted it later. Lady Lavinia jokes that it's a collector's item, because I'm fully clothed."

"He mentioned you two rode horses together in your younger days. Was he already into art back then?"

"He was constantly sketching—horses, trees, the sheep across the road. The portraits came later. I think once he moved to the Continent, that's what he was known for."

She struggled to her feet. "Guess I'll check on Lady Lavinia, and then I'll be on my way. Will you ladies let me know if you need me, please?"

Assuring her we would, we shooed her out the door and breathed a collective sigh of relief. It was Belle who spoke first. "Poor woman. She's a trouper, but she was hanging on by a thread. Now, shall we eat a bite before we start ferrying food to the family?"

We grabbed soup and sandwiches and made ourselves comfortable around the kitchen table. My friends were eager to hear how Emilia and Sophie were faring. And they were concerned about Edith.

"It's almost like Edward was a sibling," said Rhiannon. "Or perhaps a schoolmate. Clearly, they had a strong bond."

Wendy looked at Belle. "I know I'd go to pieces if Peter died. I nearly did when he had that bicycle accident."

I'd lost a mother, a father, and a husband, but not a sibling. I imagined that Wendy and Peter being twins made for a bond I'd never understand. They weren't overtly close, but she occasionally alluded to twin vibes.

There was no mention of how she was feeling, and I wondered what emotions she was concealing. "Wendy, how are you doing with this? You only met Edward two days ago, but you two got close quickly."

She cut her eyes at Belle. "Mum and I talked, and she helped me see why that happened. You know, she's not only a nurse, she's also a good listener. Then I called Rhys, and instead of beating around the bush, I told him how I felt. He listened, really listened. He wanted to drop everything and drive over here, but I convinced him that wasn't necessary."

At my skeptical look, she shrugged. "I was having a pity party because he's been so busy, and telling him about Edward's attentiveness forced me to be honest with myself and with him. That's the key to a good relationship, right? Honest communication."

Rhiannon wasn't privy to the details of Wendy's day with Edward nor of any problems with Rhys, but she listened patiently without prying. That was her way.

"So, you're okay?" I asked.

"Pretty much. Edward was engaging and attentive, but when I think about it, he revealed very little about himself. I don't know how to explain it. It was like an hours-long version of a cocktail party conversation with a charming stranger. Of course, I'm shocked. I'm sad, but I'm not devastated."

Rhiannon hit the nail on the head. "Like, 'Oh. I can't believe he's dead. He was such a nice man.' Is that what you mean?"

"Exactly." She touched my shoulder. "And how are you, Leta? I can't believe you found him."

"I didn't. Emilia did, but yes, I was right behind her. I think that Gemma's kept me so busy, I haven't had time to process the shock. And if the local constable doesn't get here soon, I'm not sure what's going to happen."

Belle leaned forward. "It's obvious, isn't it? Gemma's already leaning on you. I'm functioning as an extra family liaison officer. Ellie is close to the family, and Wendy likely knows more than she realizes. We little old ladies are perfectly positioned to offer our expertise."

Gemma popped her head into the kitchen. "What was that about the LOLs?"

Patting her white curls, Belle smiled. "We're at your disposal, Gemma."

I was completely taken aback when Gemma didn't respond with a snarky comment. She frowned as she pulled off her gloves. "What would you say if I told you I could use your help?"

Wendy glanced at me. "Leta?"

This was one for the record books. Only once before had Gemma requested my help with anything beyond observing or note-taking. That was two years ago, when her dad was a suspect in the Earl of Stow's murder. She was leaving for a two-week training course just as the investigation was kicking off with her new boss in charge.

Squinting, I studied Gemma. "I'd say you're either joking or delirious."

"Neither. I'm deadly serious."

Belle turned to me and Wendy. "Well then, girls, I'd say the LOLs are on the case."

CHAPTER TEN

WHAT GEMMA MEANT BY using our help was doling out tasks. She started with Rhiannon, who eagerly excused herself to fulfill her assignment—take a trolley filled with soup and sandwiches to the family wing. Unbeknownst to me, there was an elevator off the kitchen, so she loaded up and was gone in a flash.

When Gemma turned to Belle, I was expecting her task to be something to do with the kitchen. I thought she'd ask me to accompany her for the notification at the stables and maybe assign Wendy something similarly benign like manning the phones.

I tried to hide my smile as I noted Belle's crestfallen expression when Gemma asked her to check on Emilia. Belle had been right about being an extra FLO.

Except, there was more to Belle's assignment. "Belle," barked Gemma, "find out how long Sophie has worked for Emilia, and whether the flat in the carriage house is part of her compensation. And get Emilia to elaborate on who proposed the massage-for-painting deal with Edward and how Sophie felt about it."

Whoa. Not only had Gemma proven me wrong about what she wanted from the LOLs, she was in command mode. Trying to keep my expression blank, I waited for Belle's reaction. We often divvied up assignments among us, but not like this. No one issued orders. Gemma was dealing with several strong-willed women, and I knew this approach wouldn't work for long.

Belle crossed her arms. "You don't know how we work, do you, Gemma? We let the conversation guide us. We're opportunistic. That's why people tell us things they don't tell the police. Because we don't interrogate them, they don't see us as threatening. You're going to have to trust us to do this our way." *Way to go, Belle.*

Holding up her hands, Gemma tried to appease our resident Miss Marple. "Now, Belle, I'm not trying to tell you—"

"You most certainly are, Gemma Taylor."

Belle had succeeded in setting the tone for our interaction, so when Gemma asked me to tackle St. John, she took a more consultative approach. "What do you think we should try to find out from the viscount, Leta?"

So much for my resolve. When ideas immediately sprang to mind, it was clear I'd been fooling myself. My off-the-top-of-my-head suggestions covered where he was last night, Edward's involvement with the estate, his finances, and anything about family relationships I could glean. "I overheard something last night that will help me ease into this conversation, and then I'll follow whatever breadcrumbs he drops. And when there's time, I want to speak with Charlotte. I have a hunch I'd like to pursue."

That earned me the famous Gemma eye roll without an accompanying snarky comment. "That works, Leta. You take care of St. John and Charlotte." To say I was dumbfounded didn't capture my feelings by half. She'd invited me to snoop, and I'd stepped in with both feet.

Next, she turned to Wendy. Her assignment was to take notes while Gemma notified Rob and Annabelle. Because Wendy had spent time at the stables the previous day, Gemma thought she might be more tuned in to their reactions. They'd follow that by interviewing Bash, and then we'd regroup in the kitchen when we were done.

As I walked through the dining room with Dickens, Dave Facetimed me. I smiled as he and Christie appeared on the screen. "Hi. What are you two up to?"

"You've got to see this, Leta. We've worked out sign language for Christie. It's only two signs, but it's a start."

Christie stuck her head front and center. "It's no big deal, you know. All he had to do was ask."

"I can't wait to see. What are they?"

Dave beamed. "I feel like we need a drumroll, but here we go. Christie, do you like treats?" She swiped her nose with her paw.

I chuckled. "That must be the sign for yes. Because we know she loves treats."

"Exactly. Now, watch this. Christie, do you want dry food?"

That sign cracked me up. Her tail swished back and forth in the way of cats when they're irritated or about to pounce. "I get it. She said no."

She meowed. "Of course, I did. I want wet food, and I want it fluffed just right." She flopped and rolled on the floor. "He's been asking me silly questions like this all morning."

"Dave, this is hysterical." I told him what she'd said. "Let me try. Christie, do you miss me?" That got a nose swipe.

Dave echoed her sentiment. "We both miss you and Dickens, too. I've been listening to the weather report. Are you guys okay up there?"

Now was not the time to tell him about the murder, so I assured him we had plenty of food and firewood and wine. "And, of course, I have a good book. Got to run, sweetheart. I'll call later. Love you."

I was in luck. Bash was at the front desk. "Hi, Bash. How are you holding up?"

His face was answer enough. "Hanging in there. Better than Emilia. I think she's shell-shocked. She . . . she told me what she saw. She knows she wasn't supposed to, but she did. I haven't told anyone else."

Reaching across the desk, I grasped his forearm. "You can understand, then, why she's shocked. Hearing it secondhand is bad enough." I enquired about the rest of the family before asking where I could find his dad.

"He's in his study. In the family wing." He told me how to get there via the doorway at the left end of the upstairs hallway. "We keep it locked when the house is filled with strangers, but we didn't feel a need to do that with you here—being Ellie's friends and all."

When I entered the family wing, the first thing I saw was Rhiannon with the empty trolley. "What's your assignment, Leta? It sounded as though Gemma was on a roll."

"I drew St. John, and Bash told me his study was at the very end of the hall past the family sitting room and dining area."

She waved in that direction. "Yes, he's on his own. Ellie's still with Lavinia, and Charlotte and Emilia are eating together with Constable Atkins. Belle's with them too."

As we walked down the hall, she stopped at the elevator across from the sitting area. "I'll be back up in an hour to retrieve the dishes."

The door to the study was partially open, so I stuck my head in. He'd shoved the untouched tray of food to the far end of his desk and was staring at a jumble of papers in front of him.

He waved me and Dickens in and sat back in his chair. "Hello, Leta. Am I needed?"

"Gemma wanted me to let you know where things stand with the investigation. Her hands are full until the local constable gets here, if he does. The Scene of Crime Officers will be leaving shortly with Edward's body, and Gemma's off to notify the Thompson family at the stables. Belle and I have taken the liberty of shooing Edith from the kitchen, but no worries. We'll handle the evening meal."

There was a hint of a smile in his voice, though his face showed no signs of one. "Based on what Ellie's shared with my mother, we should be in good hands. I hear you're a dab hand with feta cheese and olives. Any chance we'll see a Greek salad tonight?"

"That's a very strong possibility, St. John."

I couldn't dive right into asking questions, so I tried a segue. "Speaking of chance, has Ellie told your mother any stories about the Little Old Ladies' Detective Agency?"

He folded his hands together on top of the desk. "Oh yes. Not only that, but Mother is suggesting that we hire you. I understand you're the ringleader, and they've nicknamed you Tuppence. Have I got that right? And I nearly forgot, there was talk of a hero dog."

"Ah yes, Dickens is part of the package, aren't you boy?" He preened and barked a yes.

It was one thing for Lady Lavinia to want our help, but quite another for the man of the house to approve. "And how do you feel about the Little Old Ladies?"

"I'm more skeptical than my mother, but as long as you don't impede the investigation, I'll follow her lead. She trusts Ellie, and that's enough for me. If involving the Little Old Ladies will make her feel she's doing everything in her power, so be it. I nearly had to swear an oath that I'd tell you everything I know. Let me caution you, though, that my mother's perspective on Edward is tinted by her rose-colored glasses. That's one reason I'm sitting here going through the debts he's run up."

All it took was the tilt of my head and a puzzled look for him to continue. "Edward was witty and charming, not to mention good-looking. Those qualities and his artistic talent attracted lots of friends—and lovers. Unfortunately, he had other less admirable traits. Let's just say that the combination earned him a few enemies."

Debts? Enemies? Enough so that someone came to Foxbourne Park to do him in?

"What does that mean, St. John?"

He rubbed his forehead. "On more than one occasion, I've had to engage a solicitor to get him out of a scrape. Some more serious than others but nearly always involving women and money."

"A scrape is a term I associate with younger men. Did Edward outgrow his penchant for scrapes?"

"If only. The last one occurred two years ago, not long after his wife died. If he got into any trouble during the five years they were together, she must have handled it. Either that, or he was more careful while he was married."

He gave me a meaningful look. "The countess was fifteen years older than my brother. I don't doubt that they genuinely cared for each other, but I think they had an understanding. She was a lovely woman, but she didn't fit the mold."

"How so?"

For the first time since I'd entered the study, he smiled. "Once Edward reached his thirties, he never once brought home a girl-friend who wasn't significantly younger. I gathered the countess had been in an unhappy marriage to a miserly older man, and her children expected her to continue leading the same reclusive life after their father died. Edward changed all that. He squired her to staid events for her charities, but he also took her to horse races, gallery openings, costume balls—things she'd never experienced. I think he gave her a new lease on life."

And she gave him money. "Are you saying Edward couldn't have afforded to do all that without her funding it?"

"Yes. And she also provided him entrée to echelons of French society he'd not previously had access to. I daresay he sold a few more paintings due to her connections."

I didn't want to leap to conclusions, but a picture was forming in my head. The countess was a respectable woman. She might take a lover behind the scenes, but she wouldn't flaunt him. Perhaps marriage was a mutually beneficial arrangement, as St. John supposed. Exposure and money for Edward, and a charming paramour for the countess.

"Leta, I imagine Charlotte knows more about their relationship than I do. She and Edward always got on. What I do know is that Edward is flat broke. The countess's money and the villas went to her children, and he ran through what little she left him.

That's why he graced us with his presence these past few months. He's never stayed this long before."

"You mean he doesn't make a living from his paintings?"

St. John rolled his eyes. "No. My brother was the epitome of a starving artist, which is one reason our father set up a small annuity for him. He knew I'd plow the necessary money into Foxbourne Park to keep it in the family, and possibly make more of it, as I have. Edward had neither the desire nor the business acumen to do any of that. Unfortunately, living within his means was not a skill Edward ever developed."

"If he needed money, why did he propose a massage-for-painting arrangement to Emilia? That doesn't make sense."

"Oh, but it does. Edward may have been an artist, but the two things he loved most in life were horses and beautiful women. If he could combine the two, all the better." St. John shook his head. "Actually, that combination was what most of his money went toward. If he wasn't riding, he was at the races. And he always had a stunning beauty on his arm. None of that comes cheap."

"You've lost me, St. John. I still don't get the massage instead of money deal."

"Sorry. My mind drifted for a moment. His old shoulder injury flared up, and Sophie's massages enabled him to continue his daily rides. Other than painting and riding, there wasn't much to keep him occupied here. Yes, he tended bar and enjoyed socializing with our guests from time to time, but it was nothing like his life on the Continent."

St. John had given me lots to ponder. I thanked him for being so forthcoming and excused myself. Downstairs, I was pleased to discover I had the kitchen to myself. That gave me time to jot notes about St. John's revelations and consider my next line of inquiry. My gut told me that Charlotte could be a wealth of information.

Wendy's voice drifted in from the back door. "It didn't seem off to you? It did to me. I could tell Annabelle was shaken, yet I felt like she wanted to say more. But every time she started to speak, either her mum or dad put an arm around her."

"You never know what you'll encounter in these situations, Wendy," said Gemma. "You're reading too much into it. You know Edward rode every day, and he was a fixture at the stables. This may well be the first time anyone Annabelle knows has died."

Gemma was snagging a cookie when her phone rang. "Hallo, Dad. What's up? Slow down. I'm not following. She was up on the ladder? Why? What was she doing on the ladder instead of you?"

Her face crumpled. "They're leaving now? Yes, I'm on my way. Not sure. Maybe an hour, depending on this storm. Yes, I'll be careful. Love you, Dad."

Patting her pockets, she started toward the dining room. "Keys. Where are my keys?"

Wendy grabbed her by the arm. "Hold on, Gemma. What's going on? Who was up on a ladder?"

Gemma turned. "Mum. She fell off. She hit her head, and they're taking her to A&E at Cheltenham. Dad needs me."

Speaking over each other, Wendy and I expressed our concern about the storm and about Gemma's state of mind. I'd never seen her like this.

"Gemma, wait, let one of us drive you," I said, just as Rhiannon sauntered through the dining room door.

She took one look at Gemma and escorted her to a chair. "Deep breaths, Gemma. Now, tell me what's going on."

We all crowded around the table as Gemma regained her composure. All she knew was that Gavin heard Libby scream and turned in time to see her tumble from the ladder. By the time the paramedics got there, she'd regained consciousness, but they were concerned enough to take her to A&E. "Remember, Leta, when you took that blow to the head and had a concussion? That's all Dad can think of. They were afraid you might have bleeding in the brain."

I recalled all too well how long it took me to recover. The way they portrayed concussions in books, you'd think they were no big deal, but I knew better. "Okay, I get it, but I don't think you should make the drive on your own, especially with the storm coming in."

Rhiannon took Gemma's hand. "There's only one thing to do. I'll go with you, and if you'll let me, I'll drive your car. That way, you can check with your dad while we're on the road. And you can stay in touch with Leta and Wendy about how things are going here."

Rhiannon was right to step in. There was no way Gemma would let me or Wendy ride with her. That would bring the investigation to a screeching halt. And, whether Gemma wanted to admit it or not, dealing with a serious injury to her mother was very different from taking charge of a similar situation when it concerned a stranger.

When Gemma quietly acquiesced, I knew she'd reached the same conclusion. I followed her upstairs and quickly located her keys as she threw clothes in her suitcase. In no time, she and Rhiannon were in the car and headed down the drive.

Wendy looked at me as I shut the door behind us. "You know what this means, don't you, Tuppence? We need to accomplish what we can before that constable gets here and shuts us down."

So much for what little resolve I had left.

CHAPTER ELEVEN

WHAT WE NEEDED WAS a place to sit and work, a room where we could read over our notes and discuss them undisturbed. When I laid that out for Bash, he suggested the drawing room. "So, you're really going to try to figure out who stabbed Uncle Edward?"

He clapped his hand to his mouth. "I know. Emilia wasn't supposed to tell me, but I'm her brother. And, of course, I've heard Ellie's tales of your exploits."

Once again, our reputation had preceded us. At this rate, we were never going to get out of the detective business. It was one thing for Belle and Ellie to work on finding missing dogs, but murderers?

I tuned back into Bash as he walked across the great hall. "You're our only guests, so let me light the fire, and it can be all yours."

A glance at the door made me feel better about that very public room. "Bash, this will work well if we can have the key. We like to scribble notes and tape paper on the walls, and we'd rather no one else saw them."

"Whatever it takes, Leta, and I think I have just the thing, left over from a corporate retreat last year." He dug through the closet on the far wall and came up with two flipchart pads and a stand. "What do you think?"

This was much better than the children's sketch pad we'd made do with in October. Now, all we needed was brainpower. I flopped on the floor in front of the fire beside Dickens. Rubbing his belly as I read my notes made that activity slightly more palatable.

Curled up in an easy chair, Wendy finished sooner than I did. "You keep reading, Leta. I'll see whether Mum and Ellie are available."

When she returned ten minutes later, I was standing in front of a blank flipchart. "Leta, they're both off duty and will be here shortly. The Foxbournes were ready to be on their own. Emilia is having a lie-down, as is Lady Lavinia, and you're going to love this—Ellie's already signed us up to work on the case. It's a good thing Gemma's off to tend to her mum."

Apparently, I was the only one who had any reluctance to get involved. This train would carry on full steam down the tracks with or without me.

"Leta, are you listening to me? I'm giving you the lay of the land. Charlotte banished the FLO to the kitchen, and Bash is off to Sophie's. He asked whether we needed anything else right now. That accounts for everyone, I think."

Bash and Sophie. Writing 'Relationships' across the top of the page, I jotted Bash and Sophie beneath it. "Wendy, I think they're boyfriend and girlfriend—or must I say partners?"

"Setting aside semantics, what makes you think that?"

"Several small things. He asked about her when Gemma notified the family. I saw him walking toward her door, and now he's off to see her. We detectives call those clues."

That got a chuckle. "Any other brilliant deductions, Miz Parker?"

"Mostly questions." I flipped to the next page and labeled it Key Questions. "Who did Edward take to dinner last night? Where did the emerald earrings come from? Who knew he was getting a massage?"

Crossing her arms, Wendy huffed. "He took someone else to dinner? That makes me wonder if he had a regular girlfriend or if he had multiple female friends." She used air quotes around the word friends.

The indignant look faded to a somber one. "He was so full of life. Handsome, charming, and attentive. Do you think it was a woman who killed him? Someone he two-timed?"

With a shake of her head, she returned to my list. "And this is the first I've heard of emerald earrings. You'll have to bring us all up to speed once Mum and Ellie get here. I can tell we're way behind."

A knock on the door heralded Ellie and Belle, and close on their heels, Constable Atkins, the FLO. She had a worried look on her face. "Do you know where Gemma is?"

Gemma left in such haste, no one had thought to tell her. When I explained, her chin trembled. "The storm is coming in quick. I . . . I need to get home."

That she would need to leave hadn't occurred to me. "Shall I call Gemma? Or is there someone else you should notify?"

"Either DI Taylor or Constable Lucas, I think. I'm told he's still at the hospital with the accident victim, and I don't see how he'll get here at all with this storm. And, if I don't leave now, I won't get home to my children. It's coming down fast."

Belle wasted no time in shooing the young woman from the room. "You go on now. We four can handle this."

After warming her hands by the fire, Ellie sat with Belle on the loveseat. "Perhaps I shouldn't be surprised, but the children are taking this much harder than their elders. Lavinia didn't come right out and say the words, but I think Edward was her prodigal son. It was as though she'd lost him long ago and had learned to treasure his sporadic returns. The constant theme was how thankful she was that her husband didn't live to see this."

I wondered whether Ellie felt the same way about her husband. Not long after his death, their eldest grandson Nicholas died.

"It's time you told me what you know, Leta. Unless that constable gets here today, we're the only hope for getting to the bottom of this. We know full well that the first forty-eight hours are critical to the investigation."

Handing Wendy the marker, I started with the revelation that Edward had been stabbed. Wendy headed a page as Crime Scene and captured the key points—from the jeweled dagger to the earrings. "Did it appear there had been a struggle, Leta?" she asked.

"That was the surprising thing to me. There was no sign of a struggle, and I wondered if he'd dozed off on the table before or during the massage." Closing my eyes, I saw the scene. "Except there wasn't any massage oil on his back, and Sophie claims she never saw him last night, but I'll get to that. And, as far as I know, only Emilia, Sophie, and Bash know how he died."

Belle and Ellie confirmed that neither Lavinia nor Charlotte seemed privy to the details, and I'd had no indication that St. John was.

Wendy looked at my brief list of questions. "Tell us about the earrings."

Explaining where I'd seen them, I brought up the photo of them on my phone. "I don't know why Edward had them, but I think they belong to Charlotte."

Wendy's mouth dropped open, a sign she had no idea why I thought that, but I could almost see the wheels turning in Belle and Ellie's heads. When Belle put her hand to her neck, I knew she had it. "The necklace. Charlotte wore an emerald necklace to dinner last night."

"Yes, and when St. John approached us at the bar, he asked where the earrings were. She said they were too ornate, and these drop earrings fit that description. Plus Sophie told us that Edward asked about a new design."

Belle tilted her head. "Because Sophie's a jeweler? But does her skill extend to something like that?"

"And more importantly," said Wendy, "what was Edward doing with Charlotte's earrings?"

From there, we supposed all kinds of things. Did St. John ask Edward to have them reset as a surprise for his wife? Or had Edward picked up on Charlotte's reluctance to wear them and taken matters into his own hands? A nice gesture, but odd. Wouldn't Charlotte want to be involved in the redesign? And in that case, why not go to Sophie directly or visit a jeweler?

"Leta," said Belle, "we've spent enough time on this. Let's set the earrings aside until you can speak with Charlotte. There may be a simple answer that will have no bearing on Edward's death. I say we discuss the potential suspects, and in my mind, the list should include anyone who lives here."

She ticked off the family members on her fingers. Lavinia, St. John, Charlotte, Bash, and Emilia. "Leta, I understand Sophie lives upstairs in the carriage house, so we need to include her too."

After jotting the names, Wendy stood back from the flip chart. "If by 'lives here,' we mean on the estate, then we need to add the Thompson family. Edith and Rob live above the stables, and Annabelle lives in one of the small cottages."

As Wendy added their names, Belle yawned. "Ladies, it will soon be time to work on dinner, and I need a bit of a lie-down. It's been a long day."

Ellie stretched her arms above her head. "She's right, you know. We need to be at our best to work through what we've observed, not only today, but since we arrived."

I was eager to keep going but agreed that some downtime couldn't hurt. Wendy tugged Belle to her feet. "Mum, I'll go upstairs with you. We probably have an hour before we need to get started. After that, Leta and I can tackle dinner, and maybe you and Ellie can capture what you know about the Foxbournes." She winked at me. "I'm sure Leta wants her usual afternoon nap, too."

On most days, she would have been spot-on. It was no secret that I loved my naps. And why I was so energized today was a mystery to me. Perhaps my perspective would change once I saw my bed.

As Dickens and I took the elevator to the honeymoon suite, I had a brainstorm. "Dickens, we're going to get Dave to help us, but first I need to tell him we've stumbled into another murder investigation."

When Dave answered my Facetime call, I could see he was still in his he-shed. He must have propped the phone on his desk, because suddenly a black head with a pink nose appeared on the screen. "Well, look at you two. Is she helping you this afternoon?"

Christie yawned. "He needs help, you know. When are you coming home?"

Having something to chuckle at was a nice change. "I think she misses me, and I wish I was there. We have a situation here."

Dave gave me a puzzled look. "That doesn't sound good. Have you lost power already? The snow is getting heavier here, but that's about it."

"The snow is the least of it, though it certainly doesn't help. We're all fine. Except there's been a murder."

The expressions flitting across his face provided a map of his thoughts. His eyes widened. His brow furrowed. He closed his eyes and sighed. When he opened them, he finally spoke. "You're very calm, so that tells me you're okay. How are the others? Especially Rhiannon. And who died?"

That told me I'd read the road map correctly. In a matter of moments, he went from shocked to worried to resigned. How like him to know I was fine and to realize that whatever the circumstances, Rhiannon might be more distressed than the rest of us. "We're all okay, even Rhiannon. She's taken it in her usual calm yogic way. Not much ruffles her. And it's Edward Foxbourne who's dead, the younger brother of the viscount."

"The one Wendy went riding with?"

"Yes, that one. Do you have time to hear the details?"

Both he and Christie assured me they did. By now, she had her paws on the desk and was listening attentively.

With Dave's questions along the way, it took nearly twenty minutes to get through an abbreviated version of the story. Several times he nudged Christie out of the way so he could jot a note. In typical Christie fashion, she nipped his hand and chastised him. "Hey, careful."

At the end, she blocked the view with her face. "If that cat's as observant as I am, he probably saw something. Have you asked him?"

"Not yet, Christie, but I will."

She screeched as Dave picked her up and moved her to the side. "I've got an idea of how I can help—but first, tell me what Christie said."

"Would you be surprised to hear she wants me to interview the cat? I will, but I'm not done interviewing humans yet. What's your idea?"

"Research. If the LOLs are handling everything, you've got your hands full, so how 'bout I Google the suspects and the victim? Unless the internet goes out, I can do that while you're cooking dinner, and I can email my notes. There should be plenty online about the Foxbourne family, and if Edward was an artist, there are probably images of his paintings and more. And give me Sophie's full name. If she sells her jewelry online, there could be a bio out there."

It was uncanny how well we knew each other. "That's exactly what I was going to ask you to do. I think St. John, Emilia, and Sophie are bound to have significant online presences. Knowing more about St. John and Emilia's businesses as well as Sophie's will be a start." I told him how Edward signed his paintings and, as an afterthought, sent him a shot of Sophie's business card.

Dave looked up from taking notes. "Who was Edward married to? Given what St. John told you, he may not have been all that successful as an artist, but he may show up in the society pages. Maybe we'll find out something that suggests a motive." I told him I'd have to ask about the wife.

We were about to sign off when Dickens jumped on the bed. "Dickens, what are you doing up here? You know you're not allowed on the bed."

"I have a question for Christie. Where is she?"

In a flash, Christie landed on the desk, scattering pens and papers. "What is it? Do you need my help?"

"Nope. We're good. I want to know why you don't just shake your head for yes and no like I do. Why swipe your nose and swish your tail?"

She stuck her nose in the air. "Silly boy. Because my way is cute, and Dave expects cute cat behavior."

I couldn't see Dave, but I could hear him. "Are they having a conversation? What did they say?"

The idea that Christie gave a hoot what Dave expected caught me completely off guard. And the fact that she was trying to be cute instead of cranky and sarcastic cracked me up. It was a struggle to stop laughing long enough to share the exchange with Dave.

"There you go, Leta. We're developing quite a relationship. Before long, we'll be communicating in whole sentences."

Months ago, when he'd recovered from the shock of learning I was a female Dr. Dolittle, he'd described his new life with me and the menagerie as a magical mystery tour. I was sure he was being overly optimistic, but if wishing could make it so, who knew?

CHAPTER TWELVE

THE RINGING OF MY phone startled me awake. I'd dozed off sitting up against the pillows with Dickens's head on my thigh. *That little Dickens. Still on the bed.*

It was Gemma with an update on Libby. "She's doing fine. You know the drill. They've started the paperwork to release her, but with this weather, we're not going anywhere soon."

She assured me her dad was holding up fine. "He's waiting until Mum feels better before he reads her the riot act. She may have to swear a blood oath that she'll never touch a ladder again. Now, tell me what's going on there. How bad is the snow?"

I walked to the window and was surprised to see the transformation. "It's a winter wonderland out there and still coming down. It's a good thing Constable Atkins left when she did. She called you, right?"

"Yes, and so did Constable Lucas. He's stuck at the hospital, and DCI Harper's still in London. At least Constable Atkins made it home to her children."

"Would you like an update?"

Did I imagine it or did Gemma just chuckle? "Indeed, I would. You and the LOLs conveniently snowed in at a country estate where there's been a murder is an image straight out of an Agatha Christie mystery. There's just one small problem—there's a very high probability the killer is snowed in with you. The idea of the four of you playing detective, without adult supervision, scares the heck out of me."

Typically, the adult supervision comment would have irked me, but I sensed genuine concern for our safety. "I'm with you, Gemma. I wish I could believe that someone snuck onto the estate to kill him, that it's not someone who lives here, but that doesn't make sense. The only saving grace is I don't think the murderer is a homicidal maniac on a killing spree. I think Edward's death was very personal, don't you?"

"Yes. But for a killer, desperate times can trigger desperate measures. You and Wendy helping with the interviews may have already put you in the killer's crosshairs. I'm asking you to stand down, as in provide comfort as appropriate, but refrain from snooping. Hopefully, you haven't already said something that worries whoever it is. If the killer thinks you know who they are, that's not good."

"But, Gemma, we *don't* know. We're grasping at straws—emerald earrings, Sophie's bejeweled dagger, Edward's debts. We can't very well let slip we know who it is when we don't."

I could almost see her rolling her eyes. "Don't act disingenuous with me, Leta Parker. Shall we name the times you've asked questions that provoked a killer? The times someone's come after you or Wendy—usually you?"

It was time for me to play my bad connection card. "Gemma, you're . . . breaking . . . up. Are you there? Darn . . . weather. . ." I hung up and turned my phone off for good measure.

She was right on several counts, but I'd been more careful lately. On the last case we were involved in, no one came after either me or Wendy. And, without us, the DI wouldn't have figured out who the killer was. I'd talk it over with Belle, Ellie, and Wendy, and we would make a joint decision on how to proceed.

In the kitchen, Wendy was chopping tomatoes and onions. "Hi there, sleepyhead. Did you have a good nap?"

"Yes. You should have texted me. Am I making a Greek salad or is all that for something else?"

"I found the ingredients for one of your Greek feasts—even phyllo dough in the freezer. You're making spanakopita and salad, and I'm your sous chef. Mum and Ellie are in the sitting room working. Please note that I've also found the wine cellar." She pointed to several bottles of red lined up on the table.

Taking the hint, I poured each of us a glass and sat down with my notebook. "Why don't you talk me through the notification of the Thompsons. You said something to Gemma earlier about Annabelle."

"Well, she took it awfully hard. I guess it fits, given that Edward took daily rides, and she saw him most days. But something in her reaction made me think it was more than that. More than a casual hello over the horses. Maybe the way we're friends with Toby." We saw Toby several mornings a week after yoga class, and we often met for drinks and dinner at the local pub. He owned the tearoom in Astonbury.

"If that's the case, she may be able to give us a fresh perspective on Edward. Not one tainted by long-time family baggage."

Her over-the-shoulder glance made me realize I hadn't shared St. John's description of Edward. I tried to make it short. "The highlights from St. John include phrases like *debt-ridden, scrapes that required a solicitor, and starving artist*. My impression is that he lived the high life while he was married to the countess, but when she died, the money dried up."

Wendy stopped chopping. "And Edith commented about the models he brought home and being fully clothed in her portrait. It caught her to a tee, but I wonder if he also painted nudes."

That was a thought. "If we knew where his studio was, we could find out." I pulled out my phone and texted Bash.

The three little dots winked as he typed his response. "Upstairs in the carriage house. I have the entry code, but Uncle Edward never locked it."

"Wendy, if you're up for an adventure, we can do some sleuthing while the casserole's in the oven."

"Who, me? When have I ever passed on an opportunity like that?"

While my sous chef finished prepping the ingredients, I retrieved our parkas. It took no time to throw two pans of spanakopita together—a layer of phyllo sheets slathered with melted butter, a layer of the spinach mixture, and a second layer of phyllo as the crowning touch. The tops would be golden brown in sixty minutes.

We ducked through the kitchen door into the falling snow. Following Bash's directions, we went to the back of the carriage house, but on the opposite end from the spa. The entry mirrored the one that led to Sophie's flat, and in the upstairs hall, a single door on the right opened to Edward's studio. I wasn't sure what I expected, but it was surprisingly tidy.

When I spied several boxes of neatly folded rags, I knew this was the room Rhubarb had shown Dickens. My next thought was that Edward had been prolific, and it dawned on me that the space held a collection that spanned at least thirty years, perhaps longer. There were landscapes, portraits, and abstracts. They were done in a mix of mediums—oil, pastels, and acrylics.

All were dated and signed E. Fox. He seemed to go through phases, both in subjects and mediums, though he often returned to an earlier style. Horses and landscapes were prominent in his younger days but were also among his more recent works.

Wendy went to two stacks of canvases propped on the far wall. "Here's my answer about nudes. Look at these. If he dated all these women, he didn't have a type. I see brunettes, blondes, and redheads; and they range from voluptuous to athletic, and from youthful to middle-aged."

Near the back of the first stack, she stopped. "It's Lady Godiva, and like the others in this stack, it's one of his earlier works."

My curiosity was piqued, and I flipped through the next stack. "These are more recent, over the last ten years, and the models are tastefully draped. Look, this is a series of one model with different colored sheer scarves. When I think about it, today's bathing suits reveal more than these subtle arrangements."

We both wandered the room. I was drawn to the portraits of riders and huntsmen. "If I'm not mistaken, this is a much younger St. John, dressed for a fox hunt. Here's another less formal image, a young woman in a Barbour jacket." There was too much to take in during the short time we had.

I thought about St. John's view of his brother. "I'm not sure that I've learned anything that will help us solve this case, but I feel as though I know Edward better. St. John painted him as a dilettante, but I sense that Edward had a real passion. It may not have paid well, but he kept at it. There's something to be said for that."

Wendy agreed. "I wonder whether Edward was the favored son. Lavinia said he was like his father, and it's easy to see that St. John followed a very different path. There could be some sibling rivalry involved. Who knows what bonds siblings or drives a wedge between them? I'm thankful that Peter and I have our twin bond despite being so very different."

When we bustled into the kitchen, we were chilled to the bone. The table was set, and Ellie was adding napkins and silverware to the rolling cart.

Belle raised her glass of wine to us. "We wondered where you'd gotten to. Based on the timer, Ellie texted Lavinia that dinner would be served in twenty minutes."

Tossing the salad took no time at all, and soon we were ready to pull the steaming pans from the oven. Wendy replaced them with a pan of rolls as I cut the spanakopita into the traditional large diamond shapes. The kitchen was equipped with covers for room service meals, so we plated the main course and stacked five meals on the cart.

Wendy and I were pushing the cart toward the elevator when the doors opened and Bash appeared. "Here, let me take that. Gran sent me down to help. That way, you can enjoy your meal while everything's piping hot. And I'll bring it all back down and help with the washing up, too."

"Bash," I said, "do you think Sophie would like a plate? I can take one over now."

He blushed. "Thanks, but she likes to eat a bit later, so I'll check then." His reaction told me I was on the right track about their relationship.

Over dinner, Wendy and I described the paintings we'd seen in the carriage house. Ellie was aware Edward painted landscapes and the occasional portrait of someone on horseback because those pieces were displayed in the manor house from time to time. The rest of what we described was news to her, however, and she was eager to see it in person. "Lavinia believes he's quite good, and, based on the little I've seen, I agree with her. Through the years, she and I have visited any number of galleries, and we both know enough about art to be dangerous."

"St. John referred to Edward as a starving artist but didn't give me any indication as to what he thought of his talent. I must admit, I'm someone who's clueless about art and buys paintings for their subject matter and colors, so hearing your perspective would be interesting."

This was as good a time as any to share the rest of my conversation with St. John. Having heard it once already, Wendy summed up when I finished. "He might not have disliked his brother, but he was definitely frustrated with him. He mentioned that Edward and Charlotte got on, but I wonder how Bash and Emilia viewed him."

Thinking back over comments I'd heard from the siblings, the perfect phrase popped into my mind. "A charming rake. That fits, doesn't it? And when I think of Edith's descriptions, rapscallion would work too."

Wendy closed her eyes as a weak smile crossed her face. "I can see him as the hero in a romance novel, on horseback, of course. And I can hear that Sade song from the '80s. He was a smooth operator, but in the moment, when he was focused on me . . . he certainly seemed sincere."

I was relieved to see how well she was holding up, given how enchanted she'd been by his rapt attention. "I don't doubt that he was, Wendy. I imagine he left a trail of broken hearts in his wake, but I don't think it would have been by design. The picture I'm getting is that he was a ladies' man whose attention was genuine, not manufactured."

Ellie smiled. "That's much how Lavinia described him. Gallant and chivalrous were words she used, and she said he'd always been at ease with himself and with others. Except for recently. On this visit, she sensed brief bouts of despondency and wondered if he was still grieving for his wife. I know what St. John said about an understanding, Leta, but that's not how Lavinia saw it."

"When I moved here from Atlanta and met all of you, it was eighteen months after Henry died, and I was still grieving. The heartache doesn't disappear overnight."

"How well I know that, Leta. Being here without Nigel hasn't been easy, as we always came together. If Lavinia and I find time to visit the hunting lodge to shoot, it will be the first time for me without him."

Whatever the reason, the issue of Edward being despondent was something I wanted to explore. He was a widower, and, according to St. John, he was nearly penniless. One or both of those things could account for his depression. I was hard-pressed to see how losing the woman he loved would lead to his murder . . . unless he had something to do with her death. *Nah. That's the stuff of fiction.*

But losing his wife did eventually lead to his being heavily in debt. And it wouldn't be the first time that someone in desperate financial straits did something stupid, like borrow money from the wrong people. But again, I was faced with the idea that someone snuck onto the estate, knew where Edward would be, and stabbed him. *Right, all I need is a villain in an overcoat and fedora.*

I volunteered to wash the dishes and suggested Wendy take Ellie to Edward's studio. Once Ellie had her overcoat, the two bundled up and were gone, leaving me and Belle to tend to the dishes. We were nearly done when we heard the rumble of the elevator.

"Leta," Bash called, "dinner was a huge hit, and Dad requested your salad for tomorrow night too."

"No problem, Bash, as long as it works with whatever Edith is planning. And if she'd like to take tomorrow off, I can always make baked ziti, or perhaps pastitsio."

I shared the story of how it had been my job to bring Greek salad to an annual Christmas dinner with friends. "We switched assignments one year, and they unanimously voted that the salad was a must-have for all future gatherings."

When he unloaded the plates, he tried to get me to make room for him at the sink.

"Bash, Belle and I have a rhythm going now. Why don't you call Sophie to see if she wants dinner, and then we can put a plate together."

Holding up his phone, he said he'd already texted her. "She may be drooling by now. She loves Greek food."

I sent him out the door with a laden tray, complete with the remaining bottle of wine. By then, Belle had brewed a pot of decaf and located a tin of cookies.

When she started to pour, I stopped her. "Let's take it to the sitting room, so we can continue working. I'll text Wendy to let her know where to find us."

I stoked the fire back to life by adding kindling and logs to the dwindling embers. Belle filled our mugs as I warmed my hands. "I'm eager to hear what you discovered by spending the afternoon with Emilia." I winked. "You followed Gemma's orders, right?"

She gave a sweet smile. "But of course. Far be it from me to disobey a direct order from our esteemed detective inspector. I did, however, let the conversation meander as usual. Emilia was quiet at first, so I simply nodded and murmured encouragement as she made random comments."

That approach typically worked well. "When I wondered aloud how Sophie was holding up, Emilia described her as a godsend. It's easy to see they're as much friends as coworkers. Technically, Emilia is the owner and the boss, but she doesn't give off that vibe."

"That's the impression I had, too. What's the backstory? How long have they known each other?"

Belle ticked off the facts. "They met five years ago when Emilia hired Sophie as a massage therapist, back when there was only one spa. In the next three years, Emilia added a spa a year, and each time sent Sophie to manage the newest. Sophie pursuing her certification as an esthetician was a boon to business."

"How did she get Sophie to leave London? I would think that this locale could be somewhat dull after living in London."

"Emilia mentioned Sophie's father being ill for a year or two and dying not long before this venture was in the works. Her dad and her job were her ties to London, and she saw this as a fresh start. The offer of the flat in the carriage house sealed the deal. It must have been hard to resist a new job with a new flat as a perk. She was already selling her jewelry in the London spas and online, and now she has a presence in the countryside. Both girls have quite the entrepreneurial spirit."

Leaving my warm spot in front of the fireplace, I started a Sophie page on the flip chart and captured Belle's findings. "Did you get any sense that Bash and Sophie are in a relationship?"

Belle's smile widened. "Oh yes. When Sophie arrived a year ago to ready the spa for its February opening, the two hit it off immediately. Emilia has high hopes that they'll get married, but for now, they're keeping a low profile."

"What does that mean?"

"The whole family knows they're an item, and they like Sophie, but Charlotte's not convinced she's the one for her son. Emilia hinted that Charlotte still holds out hope that Bash will marry a Debrett's girl. She's given up on Emilia making an appropriate match."

"You've lost me. What's a Debrett's girl?"

"Ellie could probably explain it better, but it's shorthand for an upper-class, aristocratic woman—someone from the 'right' social circle."

Why does that surprise me? Is it because St. John seems more of a businessman than a viscount? "Seriously? An aristocratic pedigree is more important than her son's happiness? I guess it's possible she thinks he could regret marrying for love, but that's hard for me to swallow."

Belle chuckled. "You have to remember, Leta, that this is merry old England. I'm sure there's a bit of this in the States with old money versus new instead of titles." I knew she was right. It was just that I thought we'd gotten beyond that kind of thing. Silly me.

"What about Emilia? Any suitors on the horizon or in the past?"

"I did manage to ask, and the answer made me wonder whether St. John or Charlotte blamed Edward for what they dubbed Emilia's poor choices in men. She lived with an artist for several years—a starving artist, if you will. Maybe her uncle's lifestyle made her more open to that kind of liaison. Wouldn't you love to be a fly on the wall for a Charlotte and St. John conversation about that? Regardless, that relationship ended before she returned to the family home."

Belle never failed to excel at gathering information, and she was especially effective with young people—as in under forty. It was her grandmotherly persona, though she'd be quick to tell you she hadn't been graced with any grandchildren. Thinking about her findings reminded me that Dave was researching the family. "Oh, my goodness. I turned my phone off before dinner. Let's call Dave to see what he's dug up."

CHAPTER THIRTEEN

WHEN I FIRED UP my phone, I was confronted with a series of increasingly irate texts from Gemma. I couldn't help smiling. "My, my, Gemma doesn't like being out of the loop. Did I mention she told me to stand down? She's worried we'll run afoul of Edward's murderer."

Belle studied my face. "You know, luv, it wouldn't be the first time. We need to be careful. Maybe we should instate a rule that we travel in pairs until an arrest is made or until we leave, whichever comes first."

"I can live with that. And I'm inclined to think it's the men we need to be wary of. The chief SOCO commented that it took considerable strength to stab Edward in the back. It's not as easy as they make it look in the movies."

Sipping her coffee, Belle looked pensive. "Narrowing it down to Bash, St. John, and Rob seems premature to me. At first blush, wouldn't you look at Sophie? She certainly fits in terms of means and opportunity."

"I can't help thinking that, too. And, as a massage therapist, she has the upper body strength to do it. But we need a motive. The closest I can come to that is something between St. John and Edward, but you don't kill your brother because he's a pain in the neck. There has to be more."

It was time to see what Dave had come up with. "If I can get through to Dave, maybe he can supply one."

Dave was on the sitting room couch when he answered my Facetime call, and once again Christie was right there with him. "Well, look at you two. Has Christie left your side since I've been gone?"

She was lying across the back of the couch peering over his shoulder, and I chuckled when she swiped her nose. I almost told her she could meow her answers for me when I remembered Belle was in the room. Hastily, I told Dave his favorite person was beside me on the loveseat.

"Hello, Belle. Are you keeping Tuppence out of trouble?"

The two bantered about me as though I wasn't there until I spoke up. "Miss Marple, here, is as likely to get into trouble as I am, and we need your help. Tell me you were successful in gathering background on our cast of characters."

"Some more than others, but I've plenty to keep you busy. Between Google and Instagram, there's a wealth of information. Let's start with the viscount. Foxbourne Holdings is mentioned in *The Financial Times* and *The Times* quite often, and from what I've read, he's a hugely successful businessman. He and his wife also appear in all the usual society columns, and *Country Life* featured him last year with a story on how he's transformed Foxbourne Park. It seems that everything he touches turns to gold."

Belle concurred. "Exactly the words Ellie used. And as she puts it, a good thing, since his father had no business sense. Was there any indication that Charlotte's involved in Foxbourne Holdings?"

"No, but she's a fundraiser for several charities and is also on the board of Roedean, where she went to school. There was mention in the *Country Life* story that she'd taken a step back recently to help the viscount with the extensive refurbishment of Foxbourne Park."

A Debrett's girl, I thought. "Emilia must have gotten her entrepreneurial spirit from her father."

"Could be. She attended Roedean like her mother, and she was a bit of a party girl, judging from the society pages and Instagram. But it looks as though she settled down pretty quickly. She was in her early twenties when she opened her first Emilia Rose spa, and she has her own line of facial products, too. Pretty impressive."

I chuckled. "It's not uncommon for a spa to develop its own line. She probably partnered with a private label manufacturer to develop it. She may have chosen from an existing line or asked them to tweak one, but that's how she'd get her name on the products. Still, it's a smart move."

"And you know this how?"

"Because the day spa I went to in Atlanta did exactly that. The owner gave me the scoop when I wrote a column about her. What about Emilia's social life? Belle found out she once dated an artist."

"Yup. I picked that up from Instagram. I think he did the murals in her first several spas, but there's no sign of recent boyfriends. Do you want to hear about Sophie Greene? She's more of a mystery woman."

My ears perked up. "You've got my full attention. Belle thinks she's our likeliest suspect, at least for the moment." I explained how means and opportunity put her at the top of the list, but that we had no clue as to a motive.

"Let's discuss what I've found and see if it helps. First, I can't find any mention of Sophie Eliza Greene until about the time she went to work for Emilia. Interestingly, that's when she first shows up on Facebook and Instagram. And those posts are all about her jewelry, nothing personal. And her jewelry is featured on the Emilia Rose accounts too."

Belle frowned. "Dave, until you made me a celebrity with your article, no one would have found me online either. And I'm not on Instagram or Facebook."

"No offense, Belle, but all the younger folks are." He winked. "Even Leta and Wendy, who are ancient compared to Sophie."

I stuck out my tongue. "As a clueless old curmudgeon, you have no room to talk. I see the mystery, though. I judge Sophie to be in her late twenties, so not being on social media until five or six years ago seems odd."

"I agree. Remember, you texted me a photo of her business card with the SEG logo? I took a shot at doing a reverse image search, and bingo, I found it. The interesting thing is that two different names are associated with it. The early images surface the name Simone Greene. Then there's a gap of several years with no sign of the logo until it appears again, this time with the name Sophie Eliza Greene."

Pulling her card from my pocket, I thought back to the conversation in her studio. "That's odd. She mentioned that her father was a jeweler who worked with fine jewelry. I wonder whether her mother's name was Simone, and she was also a jeweler. Poor girl. Both her parents are dead now."

Dave's brow furrowed. "That could be it, and if so, maybe Sophie adopted her mother's logo after she died. I'll keep digging."

"Wait. I remember now. She said her mom worked at a spa. Could Sophie have a sibling named Simone?"

Before he could reply, Belle tapped on my screen. "Dave, what did you find about Bash? Other than Sophie, we think the three men are the likeliest suspects."

"What three men, Belle? I only have St. John and Sebastian Foxbourne."

Once I explained that the third man was Rob Thompson, the stable manager, Dave went on to tell us about Bash. "He strikes me as a very down-to-earth young man. That may sound strange, given that he went to school in Switzerland, but I see him as focused and goal-oriented. He chose a path and stuck to it. He got his degree in International Hospitality Management from École Hôtelière de Lausanne and went on to work in St. Moritz at Badrutt's Palace Hotel."

His face broke into a grin. "I checked the rates thinking we could make it our honeymoon destination, but the tab for one night is nearly $2,000, so maybe not."

"I'll say. I like the idea of Switzerland, but that's ridiculous. I wonder how on earth his father enticed him to come home to run Foxbourne Park. It's lovely here, but it's not St. Moritz."

Dickens gave a yip from his position in front of the fire. "I like Bash."

With a chuckle, I reported to Dave and Belle that Dickens approved of Bash. "Dickens has spent lots of time with Bash, so maybe we should let him get the scoop."

"If the hero dog doesn't mind," joked Belle, "I'll take that assignment. Bash is an affable sort, and I bet he'll share plenty of family anecdotes once he gets started. It's also possible he'll shed more light on Sophie's background."

On my phone, I saw Christie leap from the top of the couch to Dave's lap and then stick her pink nose front and center. "Leta, enough talking. Dave needs to tend to the fire. It's getting cold in here."

It was one thing to tell Dave what she wanted. It was another to manage that in front of Belle. "Clearly, she wants something, Dave. Do you think she's hungry?"

"She's always hungry, Leta, but I just did the dab of food thing in her dish, so I don't think that's it. Hold on. Now she's trying to tuck herself beneath my sweater. Maybe she's cold."

It wasn't long before he figured it out. "Oh, I need to stoke the fire. I'll do that and then get back to my research. Talk later?"

When Belle commented that Dave was getting better at understanding Christie, I had to keep myself from bursting into laughter. Little did she know.

CHAPTER FOURTEEN

I WAS CONTEMPLATING FETCHING a bottle of Kahlua from the bar when Gemma called. "Finally! I was beginning to think a cell tower was down. Probably just overloaded."

Rolling my eyes, I didn't disabuse her of that notion. "Glad you got through. How's your mom? Did you guys make it home?"

"It was a nightmare drive, but we made it. She's ensconced on the couch in front of the fireplace, and Paddington is curled up in her lap. After giving Mum a lecture she won't soon forget, Dad's making us hot spiced cider and muffins. Now, tell me how things are over there."

When I put her on speakerphone, Belle filled her in about making dinner for the family and enjoying the bright fire in the sitting room. She made it sound as though that was all we'd been up to, but Gemma didn't fall for it.

"How naïve do you two think I am? I'm sure you did what you do best—snooping in the guise of comforting—despite what I told you. Tell me what you've found out while I've been playing nurse."

Again, I let Belle take the lead, and Gemma complimented her on completing the task she'd been assigned, getting the backstory on Emilia and Sophie. The one thing that surprised her was the Sophie and Bash connection. She hadn't picked up on that.

When it was my turn, she homed in on St. John's description of Edward. "Sounds like the prodigal son is an apt description. Bash alluded to his uncle's love for the ladies, but now we have a more complete picture. Constable James is snowed in at the Stow police station, so I'll get him to dig into Edward's background. If St. John had to hire a solicitor, there may be a record on our database. In fact, since Edward had a home in Paris, I'll also get him to check with the Préfecture de Police on the off chance any of his scrapes happened there."

"Gemma," I said, "does this change your opinion as to whether the killer is a member of the family? If Edward's death is tied to his past and someone snuck onto the estate, they would have to be long gone, don't you think?"

"I still think an outsider is an unlikely scenario, but I have to consider it. And, Leta, if you're asking if you can continue digging, the answer is still no. Provide comfort and support. That's it."

I couldn't use the bad connection ploy a second time. "Then it's time for me to sip some Kahlua in front of the fireplace and read my book. It's been a long day."

As I'd intended, she took me to mean that I understood snooping was off the table, and said she'd be in touch the next day. It was my good fortune that she was off her game after

Libby's accident. As long as Libby was doing well, Gemma being distracted was fine by me.

"Belle, that went well—shall I grab the Kahlua, along with four glasses, so the LOLs can continue comparing notes? Wendy and Ellie should be back soon." Her ready nod sent me on my way.

With no fire going, the bar was unbelievably chilly. I hastily found the liqueur and glasses and headed back to the warmth of the sitting room. It was perfect timing when Ellie approached from the dining room. "Here, let me help you with the door. That Kahlua is a welcome sight."

Belle glanced over her shoulder as we entered. "Just in time. The only thing we need now is a fresh pot of coffee."

"Coming right up," I said. "Ellie, did you lose Wendy?"

"She's in the kitchen on the phone with Rhys. And, Leta, some biscuits would be good too."

I heard Rhys's voice when I opened the kitchen door. "The name's familiar, but I don't know why. I'll Google it when we're off the phone, and I can also ask around."

Seeing Wendy's expression, I assumed she and Rhys were once again seeing eye to eye. He was one of my favorite people, so I hoped it was more than a temporary reconciliation.

"Thank you, darling. Leta's come to fetch me, so I have to run. If you find anything significant tonight, please ring me back."

As I made coffee, Wendy prepared a plate of cookies. "Rhys has a vague notion he's heard of Edward Foxbourne, or possibly Edward Fox. His forte is Golden Age authors, but he knows a bit about art too, so perhaps he'll come up with something."

She waited until we were settled in the sitting room with our coffee and Kahlua to reveal that she and Ellie had made a discovery in Edward's studio.

I chuckled when Belle chided her. "Well, don't keep us waiting, girl. What was it?"

"Leta and I never thought to look at the painting on Edward's easel. It looked as though Edward had hastily thrown a cloth over it, just like in the movies." She pointed toward Ellie. "But that didn't deter our dowager countess."

Ellie ducked her head. "I couldn't see a reason not to. Someone was bound to uncover it sooner or later. Why not us?"

"This is great dramatic effect," I said, "but I'm dying to know what it was."

After humming Chad and Jeremy's "Lady Godiva," Wendy described the painting. "It wasn't like the nudes we saw with scarves. It was a woman on horseback dressed in a riding outfit—breeches, boots, and a red jacket. The only Godiva touch was that the white blouse beneath the jacket was unbuttoned nearly to her tummy and hinted at the curve of her breasts. It was suggestive yet tasteful."

"And rather well done," added Ellie. "The mystery is that it's incomplete. He hadn't started on the face yet."

She preened when Wendy pointed at her. "But, thanks to Ellie, we have a few guesses. Tell them, Ellie."

"As I wandered around the room, I found stacks of pencil and charcoal sketches of various subjects, but my best find was a sketchpad filled with faces. There were dozens of sketches, all of different women. On a few, he'd drawn in the collar of a riding jacket, as though he was deciding which model would be in the finished painting. You'll never guess the faces we saw."

I started checking off women we'd met since we'd arrived. "If you recognized the face, it must be someone here at Foxbourne Park. Don't keep us in suspense. Who was it?"

Wendy put one hand on her hip and tapped her chin with the other. "It was faces—plural— as in more than one. And we didn't recognize them all."

"Based on what we've heard about Edward and younger women, my guess would be Sophie and Emilia. But would he feature his niece in a painting like that?"

"Was one of them Annabelle?" said Belle.

"Yes, Mum. You and Leta have named the three we knew. There were several others we didn't recognize, and we wondered if they were some of the staff that aren't here now, or perhaps a local or two."

I looked at Belle. "Annabelle would make the most sense. She's the horsewoman in the group."

A flurry of images ran through my brain and ended with one of my petite platinum blonde friend as the model. "I wonder, Wendy, whether Edward had it in his head to paint a portrait of you in the same pose."

"I'd be flattered if he did. Ellie found two sketches of me, but they were from the waist up. If his family doesn't mind, I'd like to have them."

Belle looked at her daughter. "If there are two, you should give one to Rhys. He'd like that."

A kernel of an idea was forming in my head. "Ellie, did any one face appear more often than the others?"

"I didn't count them, but let me think." She closed her eyes as though seeing the sketch pad. "If I had to guess, I'd say there were more of Annabelle than of Sophie and Emilia. Since the others weren't familiar to me, I didn't pay much attention to them."

As she often did, Wendy seemed to read my mind. "If that's the case, it could explain why she seemed so upset when Gemma and I met with her and her parents. She not only saw Edward regularly at the stables, she also modeled for him."

This back and forth brought an obvious question to mind. "Wendy, Edward didn't get beyond flirting with you, but he might have, given time. Don't you wonder what his relationship with Annabelle was?"

"I didn't until I just now replayed her reaction to the news of his death. Think about it. Was she only a model, or also a friend, or a lover, or all three? If we're listing suspects in rank order, it moves Annabelle higher."

It was time to start a page for Annabelle, but before I could get beyond her name at the top of the page, there was a knock on the door. Wendy leaped up and disappeared into the hallway to speak with whoever it was, while I quickly flipped to a blank page to keep our brainstorming concealed.

The door opened wide to reveal Bash. "Leta, I wanted to catch you before I forgot. Sophie would like your spanakopita recipe. She thought she'd make a pan for us to share with Annabelle and Emilia one night. We four try to get together for game night every few weeks. We're hooked on Exploding Kittens right now."

"Exploding Kittens? Do I even want to know? But no worries, I'll jot it down for you. By the way, do you have Edith's cell number? We should let her know we're willing to handle breakfast tomorrow morning. No need for her to trudge through the snow."

He asked for my number and texted Edith's to me. "Leta, if you ladies are good with simple eggs, potatoes, and toast, we certainly don't require anything more than that upstairs. Ring me in the morning, and we'll come up with a simple plan. You've already gone above and beyond."

Wendy wasted no time once Bash departed. She quickly jotted several key points on Annabelle's page. Friends with Emilia, Bash, and Sophie. Edward's model—was it more? Upper body strength. Motive—jealousy?

With a yawn, I considered her list. "Wendy, who would she be jealous of? You?"

"I doubt it, but maybe she thought Edward had something more than massages going with Sophie. Except if jealousy was her motive, she'd kill the other woman, not Edward, right? And if Bash and Sophie really are a couple, she'd know better."

Her comment about Sophie and Bash made me realize that she and Ellie had missed out on the earlier conversation because they'd been in Sophie's studio.

Belle must have realized that too. "Leta, we're not all on the same page. Why don't you bring Wendy up to speed about our discussion tonight, and Ellie, too, if she can keep her eyes open. I'm off to bed."

When Ellie indicated she could stay for another hour, Wendy escorted Belle to the elevator, and I tried to organize my thoughts. As succinctly as possible, I needed to cover my, Belle's, and Dave's findings about St. John, Charlotte, Edward, Emilia, Sophie, and Bash. Doing that in an hour was going to be a challenge.

Ellie sipped Kahlua while I completed pages for the family, starting with Emilia and Bash. Their relationship with Edward seemed the least complicated. Other than Bash having the physical strength to plunge a dagger in Edward's back, nothing made me want to put either of them near the top of the list. I smiled as I jotted "Sophie's boyfriend" on Bash's page.

Charlotte's details were also easy to capture. The earrings were my big question about her. Were they hers, or only a close match? Why did Edward have them? And St. John had said that Edward and Charlotte got on, so how close where they? Could she shed light on his other relationships?

As I studied my notes on Charlotte, Ellie voiced what I was thinking. "What we know about Charlotte is more about her social standing than anything personal, isn't it?"

"How well do you know her, Ellie?"

"Not well, at all. Nigel and I spent more time with Lavinia and her husband than we did with St. John and Charlotte. They were often in London or elsewhere until St. John became the viscount. That's when the two moved back here. Perhaps you'll learn more when you ask her about Edward and his countess."

"And the emerald earrings. Unless they're not hers—in which case, it will be a short conversation."

Turning back to the flip chart, I considered what I knew about St. John. For me, he was a more complex subject. Dave had supplied details about his business success, which seemed above board. His feelings for his brother were the issue. Was Edward more than a minor irritant? Was he on his way to causing significant embarrassment for the Foxbourne family? Enough so that St. John would want him out of the way? And the SOCO would say that St. John fit the bill for the required upper body strength.

That's where I was when Wendy returned. "Well, you've been busy. Mum said you had plenty to share."

Suggesting that she work her way through the four family pages that were now displayed around the room, I tackled what I knew about Edward. What a tale. Married to a wealthy countess. Brought home any number of beautiful women. Often in debt. Shoulder injury. Horseman. Who did he have dinner with the night he died? The earrings. What was his relationship with Sophie? Did he have a local girlfriend? Was it Annabelle? Massage-for-paintings arrangement. Horses, debts, women.

Wendy came to my side as I wrote. "So many of the notes are normal, so to speak, but then you get to Edward. His life really is the stuff of fiction."

"I think that's an apt description. And not a bad life, until his untimely demise."

By now, Ellie was walking around the room perusing the notes. "I've got a few things to add. Whether or not any of it's useful, I can't say. Some of it I already knew. For example, Edward's wife Marguerite was the Dowager Countess de la Roche-Forêt. I wonder whether she disliked being referred to as a dowager as much as I do."

I jotted down the name. "That could be useful, Ellie. It might help us find mention of her and Edward in the society pages in France, and I should let Gemma know. She has Jonas researching Edward's scrapes. To me, the word scrapes makes whatever he did sound like childhood pranks, but I suspect they were more than that. Anyway, what else do you have?"

"Only that he was riding with Edith when he injured his shoulder all those years ago. His horse threw him, and it was Edith who rode back to the stables to get Rob so he could pick him up and get him back to the house. I imagine it would have been a long painful walk, if she hadn't been with him."

"No wonder this is so hard on her," I said. "They've been friends forever."

"Oh, and that note about Sophie and Bash. Lavinia thinks Charlotte's being ridiculous about it. Her perspective is that he's head over heels, and he hasn't been that way over anyone since he was in college. Lavinia's ready to plan a wedding."

At Wendy's confused look, I explained that Charlotte hoped Bash would marry someone with the appropriate pedigree for a someday viscount. We were both in Lavinia's camp.

"And that brings us to Sophie," I said. "Dave dubbed her a mystery."

After jotting several bullet points, I elaborated on his findings and what I'd learned on my own. "Ladies, what questions does this raise for you?"

Ellie led off. "If she didn't appear on social media until five years ago, was she hiding something? Who is Simone Eliza Green? Her mother, her sister? And why did Edward think she could reset the emeralds?"

Scrunching her mouth to the side, Wendy summed up. "Dave's right. There's something there. And, Leta, you're the best person to figure it out."

"True. I've begun building a rapport with her, and heck, she wants my recipe. I'll tackle her in the morning. Now, let's get these pages taped to the wall so I can get to bed."

When we were done tearing and taping, Ellie stood in front of Charlotte's page. "You know, formal portraits of all the viscounts and viscountesses are hanging on the wall in the library. What are the chances Charlotte's wearing her emeralds in her portrait?"

With a squeal, Wendy hugged her. "Ellie, that's brilliant. If we know for sure the earrings are hers, we'd be better armed to ask Charlotte what's up. I still can't fathom why Edward would have them."

"And that information could change what I say to Sophie. I'm tired, but I won't be able to sleep until we check."

We traipsed to the library, where Ellie directed us to the wall on the right, opposite the bar. Centered on the wall was a landscape featuring the gazebo and the pond. To its left were portraits of the first viscount and his early descendants. Those to the right were more recent. All had brass plaques affixed to the lower part of the frame, and small lights on the top.

With bated breath, I approached Charlotte's portrait. "They're here! She's wearing the choker and earrings."

Wendy grasped my arm. "Where's your phone, Leta? With the photos from the spa?"

Holding my phone up to the painting, I compared the earrings. "There's no doubt. Edward had Charlotte's emeralds. But why?" I snapped a shot of Charlotte's ear.

The corners of Wendy's mouth turned up. "Doesn't matter why. It's a clue, and we're a step closer to figuring this out." Wendy was ever the optimist.

It was Ellie who took the wind out of her sails. "Or, in the spirit of Dame Agatha, a red herring."

I threw up my hands. "We've been on this roller coaster before. I say we call it a night and see what the morning brings."

A neon sign pointing to the murderer would do the trick.

CHAPTER FIFTEEN

MENTALLY THANKING BASH FOR the warmth of the fire that greeted me in my room, I made quick work of readying myself for bed. I promised myself I'd read only a few pages in my book as I texted Dave goodnight. *No dice.* The real-life murder mystery kept intruding upon my thoughts.

After rereading the same paragraph multiple times, I gave up, turned out the light, and allowed my brain to rewind the tape of the evening. Sophie and Charlotte were priorities for the next day but speaking with Annabelle was too. I was puzzling over the nature of her relationship with Edward when my Billy Joel ringtone sounded.

"Hello, Tommy. Have you called to say goodnight, or have you cracked the case from afar?"

As usual, my calling him Tommy elicited a chuckle. "A bit of both, Tuppence. I wouldn't have called this late if not for your text. What are you doing up at this hour?"

"The evening got away from us, perhaps because the idea of being snowed in with a killer gave us a sense of urgency. Who knows? The good news is we've captured what we know so far. The bad news is we have lots of blanks to fill in. There are too many unknowns about Annabelle, Charlotte, and Sophie."

His fingers tapped in the background. "That was a drumroll, Tuppence. I've accidentally found out something about Sophie."

"How do you find information accidentally?"

"You know how Google fills in letters when you use the search bar? I was fiddling around with SEG and Simone Green when the name Simon Elgar Green popped up. He may be her father."

"Oh! She told me he was a jeweler but didn't mention his name. Could Simone be a sister who also followed in her father's footsteps as a jeweler? Simon, Simone, and Sophie Green, a family of jewelers?"

"It's more sinister than that. There's no sign of a sister. I think Sophie and Simone are the same person, and Simone changed her name to Sophie because her father went to prison."

I sat up in bed and turned on the light. "What? What for?"

"I hope you're sitting down. Receiving stolen property and conspiracy to commit fraud."

As I sat stunned, he explained that the details were all over the papers at the time. "Thieves brought him stolen jewelry to recut or reset so they could sell it on—we're talking diamond chokers and such. He sometimes created paste versions of the pieces. I'm not clear about whether he also sold the stolen jewelry in his shop, but he was part of the scheme, for sure."

"I'm picturing Cary Grant in *To Catch a Thief*, except Simon wasn't the cat burglar, was he?"

"Right, though the story has the makings of a book or a movie. Would you believe that his father got his start legitimately making paste copies for the nobility? I mean I guess you'd call it legitimate. Picture a cash-strapped count or duke bringing him an expensive piece to recreate so he could sell the original to raise funds. In that scenario, the wife would be unaware that she was wearing a fake. I don't suppose there's a law against that. And Simon carried on the family tradition, except with stolen goods."

"Are you saying that Sophie, or Simone, helped him? Did Sophie go to prison, too?"

There was that gentle chuckle again. "Patience, grasshopper. I don't have all the answers yet, but I haven't found any mention that she did."

If our routine reference to old mysteries was any sign, we were two peas in a pod, or at least two peas of the same age. I didn't know many people who regularly mentioned Agatha Christie's Tommy and Tuppence. And I wondered who besides us would know where the grasshopper phrase came from.

A smile stayed on my face as I listened to the rest of Dave's explanation. "It's possible that her father protected her as he did the thieves he worked with. That's why I say it could be a movie. He refused to name names. If he had, his sentence would have been much lighter. Instead, he got the maximum—fifteen years."

When I added these revelations to what I already knew about Sophie, a backstory began to emerge. "I'm thinking aloud here, Dave, so bear with me. The logo SEG, along with the name Simone Green, dropped off the radar several years ago. The logo reappeared attached to the name Sophie Eliza Green. That scenario would work if the daughter went to prison and took on another identity when she got out. Or she may simply have chosen to change her identity because her father's name was all over the papers, not because she had anything to do with the crime."

I blew out an exasperated breath. "There are too many possibilities to parse without more information."

"I've been analyzing the tale for an hour, so let me try. Her father was convicted ten years ago, but he died in prison after four years. So he died six years ago, and it was shortly after that the name Sophie Green appeared. I bet she was a teenager when her dad was convicted, and she may have been innocent of any crime. On the other hand, if she was part of the family business, so to speak, he would have protected her. If he didn't give up the names of the thieves, he certainly wouldn't have given up his daughter."

"You know, you're making my head hurt."

"Sorry about that. If only I were there, I could map it all out. As it is, none of us are going anywhere. Is it still coming down there? It tapered off here and then started up again. The quiet is heavenly, though."

Sliding my feet into my slippers, I moved to the glass doors. "I wish you could see the view from my room. It's like a postcard or a scene in that Bing Crosby movie, *White Christmas*. And, yes, it's still coming down."

"White Christmas. I wonder if we'll have a white wedding?"

"I'm afraid to wish for that in case it's as bad as this. A gentle sprinkle of snow would be beautiful, but not a major storm."

I was saying goodnight when he interrupted me. "Wait. Something else popped into my head today. Do you remember the first time you told me you loved me?"

"How could I forget?" It was over the phone six months after we'd met, and I'd been trying to explain why I'd been putting him off about visiting. It all boiled down to my worry that this thing between us wasn't real, that it had happened too quickly. When he'd gently asked, "What are your concerns, Leta?" my response had been less than eloquent. "Oh hell, I love you," I'd blurted.

"What if we wrote our own vows and that was part of it?"

I nearly choked. "You're not serious!"

He laughed so hard, he was gasping. "Not at all. But admit it, I had you going for a moment. I was wondering whether we should write our own vows, and your romantic words came to mind. I'm realizing, though, that I'm pretty traditional. Setting aside those out-of-step words about promising to obey, are you okay with to love and to honor? I kind of like those."

Lord, how I love this man. "Absolutely. I want 'Here Comes the Bride' and the 'Wedding March,' and a short, traditional ceremony."

When I tried unsuccessfully to stifle a yawn, Dave knew his time was up. We said our goodnights, and I stoked the fire and rubbed Dickens's warm belly. His only reaction was to raise his head and open one eye. It was tempting to wrap up in a blanket and join him, but I opted for bed.

Picturing the winter wonderland outside my room, I turned my thoughts to a December wedding with a storybook setting, and it wasn't long before I drifted off to sleep.

It was still dark when Dickens nudged my hand. "Leta, wake up. I need to go out."

A glance at my phone told me it was 6:30, and I groaned. "Need or want, Dickens? Can't I sleep a little longer?"

"What does that mean? Let's go."

I should have realized that Dickens couldn't appreciate the distinction. And at home, Dave would have taken him out by now. Stumbling out of bed, I moved as fast as I could. I was soon bundled up and headed downstairs with Dickens prancing impatiently by my side. The aroma of coffee greeted me as I tugged at the front door, and I glanced toward the dining room, tempted to grab a mug before we went out.

"No time, Leta. Got to go."

Dickens darted down the stone steps, but I held on to the railing as I gingerly made my way. He was a fastidious little thing, and I was pleased to see him run to a clump of trees that edged the gravel area. Only his pawprints disturbed the carpet of snow that greeted me. It really was a winter wonderland. With my and Ellie's cars stowed in the carriage house, I could almost imagine we'd traveled back in time. Had a horse-drawn carriage appeared in the distance, it would have been perfect.

Following Dickens as he wandered around the carriage house, I saw footprints heading toward the kitchen door. Sure enough, that's where they stopped.

When I put my hand on the doorknob, Dickens barked. "Do we have to go in, Leta? Can't we take a walk?"

"How 'bout you wander while I get coffee?" The words were barely out of my mouth before he took off.

Leaving my boots by the bench inside, I undid my parka and followed my nose. The aroma of coffee was joined by that of bacon frying, and I realized I was ravenous. "Good morning, Edith."

Edith glanced my way as she pulled a loaf of bread from the oven. "Thought that was you when I heard the bark. Is Dickens behind you?"

"He would be if he knew there was bacon. He's romping in the snow for now." I pulled my cloche from my head and shook out my hair. "How are you this morning?"

"As well as can be expected. Keeping busy helps."

She put another loaf in the oven. "Thanks for your kindness yesterday. Knowing dinner was taken care of was a huge relief. St. John popped down this morning to tell me I must get your salad recipe, and Bash raved about the spanakopita when he called me last night. Said you'd handle breakfast, too, but no need. I'm serving a full English today."

She bustled around while I shed my coat and poured coffee. Glancing at my phone, I saw that I'd missed two texts, one from Wendy and another from Gemma. The reply to Wendy was the simpler of the two. When I typed that I was in the kitchen and asked if she wanted to take a walk, I got an immediate thumbs-up.

Gemma wanted me to call her with an update, not something I could do in front of Edith. I expected an impatient response to my putting her off, but she was surprisingly calm. Constable James had information about Edward, and I should call him when I was free. She was helping her dad with breakfast and firewood and would be busy for a bit.

Speaking directly with Jonas had its advantages. That meant I'd get the unfiltered story rather than only the facts Gemma thought I needed. I was on my second cup when Wendy came in from the dining room. She went straight to Edith and gave her a comforting hug before turning to me. "I've been drinking coffee for what seems like hours. Shall we take that walk now?"

As we left through the side door, Dickens and Lucky came bounding toward us from the gazebo. They pranced in anticipation as I formed a snowball and darted off when I tossed it. When Wendy followed suit, they were in heaven.

As we walked toward the gazebo, I shared Dave's discovery about Sophie. "That story makes me want to speak with her first thing. I haven't seen any lights in the carriage house, so she must not be up yet. I know it's a stretch, but I can't help wondering whether Edward asking her about those earrings has any connection to her past . . . to her father."

"I hadn't gotten that far. It's possible, I guess. But a simpler explanation is that he recognized her expertise without knowing anything of her past."

I dusted snow from my gloves. "What I need to find out is how involved she was with her father's criminal activities, if at all. I'll see what she says, and then maybe Gemma or Jonas can do a deeper dive to verify her story."

"You know, Leta, catching her before she's fully awake could work to your advantage. If the light's on when we get back, why don't you meet with her. I can call Jonas about Edward, and then we can decide how to handle Charlotte and Annabelle. Don't you wonder whether Sophie's aware that those earrings are Charlotte's?"

"I wonder lots of things." We'd been walking side by side, but I turned to face her. "Has it occurred to you that Edward and Charlotte might have had a connection beyond brother- and sister-in-law—that they might have been having an affair?"

When her mouth dropped open, I knew it hadn't. "Why on earth would you think that?"

As I laid out the details that prompted the idea, I ticked them off on my fingers. "He's a womanizer. She's attractive—though, knowing his taste, possibly a bit old for him. Maybe they had an affair years ago or maybe it's recent. And he had her earrings. Did she leave them in his room, or did he pick them up when he was in hers?"

She blew out her breath. "I can buy the possibility they had an affair, but that doesn't explain why he'd have her earrings."

Thinking aloud, I built on the idea of an affair. "You're right, though an affair would make St. John a strong suspect. Getting rid of your pain-in-the-neck brother who just happened to be cuckolding you would be a twofer. It's the strongest motive we've come up with. For that the matter, it's the only one."

We turned toward the manor house, each deep in our own thoughts, until Lucky shot past us and Dickens slid to a stop. "Look, Leta, it's Sophie. Do you think she has snowballs too?"

"You're out early, Sophie," I called.

Continuing past her door, she approached us, a tentative smile on her face. "So are you. Any chance you're in charge of breakfast this morning? If so, I'll be right over. If it's anything like last night's dinner, I don't want to miss it."

Wendy told her I had the morning off. "But Edith's fixing a full English."

"Nothing against Edith's cooking, but I was imagining a Mediterranean delight like a spinach and feta omelet. You can't find those in Deddington."

"Maybe Edith will let me do tomorrow's breakfast." I knelt to scoop a handful of snow for a snowball. "Did you walk to the stables this morning? That's quite a trek."

"No. I spent the night with Annabelle. She didn't want to be alone, and she didn't want her parents hovering over her."

Wendy peeled off toward the kitchen door, leaving me and Dickens with Sophie. *Might as well tackle this head-on.* "Sophie, do you have time to chat with me now? I'm hoping you can fill in some blanks for me."

It was clear I'd caught her off guard, but she invited me up to her flat anyway, albeit reluctantly. "I'll make coffee or tea, if you prefer."

"Coffee's fine by me," I said as she unlocked the downstairs entrance. In her flat, Rhubarb meowed a greeting and a request for food. Only after that did he rub noses with Dickens.

"He must be hungry since you've been gone all night, but his meows are nothing like my cat's. When she accosts me in the morning, you can almost hear her saying, 'I want food, now!' The tone is a dead giveaway."

"Rhubarb's rarely demanding, and if he is, it's about wanting to go out. He was feral when he started hanging around my flat in London, and he loves it here."

While we waited for the coffee to brew, Sophie built a fire in her wood-burning stove. Dickens and Rhubarb wasted no time before curling up together on the fluffy rug in front of it.

Sophie handed me a cup of coffee and motioned me toward the couch. "I've told you everything I know, Leta, so this shouldn't take long."

"Maybe longer than you think, Sophie. I'm curious. Why did you change your name?"

Her eyes widened as her mouth dropped open. I'd taken her by surprise. "What do you mean?"

I fudged a little. "I was thinking of having you make bridesmaids' gifts for me and asked my fiancé to Google you." *Like I have any plans to have bridesmaids.* "He stumbled across your SEG logo, but it was for a Simone Green. That can't be a coincidence."

"Oh, I never liked my name . . ."

Holding my hand up, I stopped her midstream. "Sophie, he also found a Simon Green. Is that your father?"

It was clear I'd caught her off guard, but she recovered with an indignant tone. "What does my name have to do with anything?"

When I didn't respond, her demeanor changed. It was though she was a beat behind me, as though my mention of her father had taken a moment to sink in.

Sagging against the couch, she whispered, "You . . . you know about my father?"

At my nod, she looked down at her hands. "I've done everything I can to put that behind me. It . . . it was a nightmare. I told myself it had to be a mistake, that it couldn't be true. My father couldn't possibly be a criminal. It was all over the papers, and it took no time for people to figure out I was his daughter. My manager at the gift shop said she had no choice but to let me go. And she stopped carrying my jewelry. I lost my job. My friends stopped calling. I sold my jewelry at weekend markets, but I was barely scraping by."

"Did changing your name help?"

"Yes. I finally realized that if I was going to reclaim my life, there was no other way. The name change meant I could apply for better jobs with no questions asked. And I pursued massage therapy because of Mum. It always interested me, and the time was right."

Given the story that was pouring out, I didn't need to ask whether she'd gone to prison. That didn't mean she wasn't involved in the scam or the fraud, but I had to ask. "Sophie, did you help your father remake or reconfigure the stolen jewelry?"

I knew I'd struck a nerve when she leaped to her feet. "No! I can't believe you're asking me that. I had no idea until he was arrested."

Suddenly, tears formed in her eyes. "All those hours with him in the shop, I was blind to what was going on, and he never offered me an explanation. He only said he was sorry over and over again. It took a long time . . . a very long time for me to forgive him. I miss him but I'm also angry with him. Because of what he did, I didn't get to spend the last few years of his life with him. It was only a few years after he went to prison that he got cancer."

After a moment of silence, I shifted gears. "Tell me about the emerald earrings."

She gave me a sharp glance. "I already told you. Edward wanted me to come up with a design. That's all."

"Somehow, Sophie, I think there's more to it. Had you done that for him before?"

Coffee sloshed from her cup. "Yes. He made me."

"Made you draw a design? Or something else?" My question hung in the air.

"It started with the design. I knew he was widower, and when he came to me with his wife's sapphire choker, I was happy to help. He said he was considering having it made into two necklaces for her daughters, and I was flattered that he liked my work enough to ask my opinion. Still, I was a tiny bit worried he was after something. And I was right."

She shuddered. "He described my design as exquisite and asked if I could recommend a local jeweler to do the work. When I suggested two jewelers in Oxford, he gave me a strange smile, and I *knew*. I knew what was coming. 'If you're as good as your father,' he said, 'you'll do an excellent job.' I was a fool to think he wouldn't know who I was."

"Sophie, how did Edward know?"

"I was a teenager with braces back then, and prayed he wouldn't remember me, but I recognized him right away."

The look on my face must have told her she'd lost me. "He reminded me of Orlando Bloom in *Lord of the Rings*, and I was half in love with him. If anything, he was more handsome now than he was then. I never wondered why he spent time with Dad in the back workroom. It was much later that I figured out he was one of them."

"One of who?"

"Jewel thieves, burglars, whatever you want to call them. They supplied the jewelry that my father worked with. He never gave up any of his accomplices, but I pieced together who some of them were. I remember the discussions about whether it was better to recut or reset the beautiful stones. Not everyone took the time to offer suggestions, but Edward always did."

"Edward? Edward was a jewel thief?" I'd considered all kinds of possibilities, but not this one. In a way, it made sense. If he was a starving artist, as St. John described him, he needed another means to support his lifestyle.

When Sophie nodded, I asked the logical question. "Was he stealing from the guests here at Foxbourne Park?"

"I don't know! I was suspicious, but what could I do? He brought me three pieces in all, claiming they were his wife's. I didn't want to ask too many questions, and I did as he asked. I had no choice."

"What do you mean?"

"I tried to tell him I wasn't my father, that I couldn't help him. He offered me money to do the work, and when that didn't work, he threatened me."

Until she uttered the word *threatened*, I had begun to imagine him as a handsome, charming cat burglar à la Cary Grant. "Threatened you? Did he hurt you, Sophie?"

The stricken look on her face made me fear the worst. "No! He said . . . he said, 'perhaps you'd accept my silence as payment.' If I didn't do as he asked, he would tell Bash and his parents about my father. Charlotte was already unhappy about me and Bash. Emilia might have stood up for me, and Bash might have forgiven me for keeping it from him. But Charlotte would have won out, and I'd have lost Bash *and* my job."

"Sophie, how much did he pay you in the end?"

"Not a penny! I told him I wouldn't accept his money. I couldn't have lived with myself if I had."

Tears streamed down her face. "It was months ago that he brought me the last piece, and with him planning to leave in the spring, I hoped that would be it. Until he started in about the earrings."

She picked up her phone. "And when he sent the photo, I knew! I knew they were Charlotte's. How could he steal from his own sister-in-law?"

By now, she was sobbing uncontrollably. "That's why I ignored his text. I couldn't think. If I didn't do what he asked, he would ruin my life. Should I tell Bash about my father? Would he still love me? If I told him about his uncle, would he believe me? Was there any way out?"

Was her answer to commit murder? Was it Sophie who stabbed Edward as he lay on her massage table?

CHAPTER SIXTEEN

I WASN'T ABOUT TO ask her that question. All too many times, I'd inadvertently put myself in danger, so I rubbed her back and shushed her while I considered what to do. As her tears slowed, she curled herself into a ball on the couch. Rhubarb joined her and licked her face, and Dickens nuzzled her hand.

After spreading a blanket over her, I stood staring out the window at the treetops covered in snow. What I wouldn't give to enjoy the peaceful scene without thoughts of murder intruding.

The sound of Sophie snoring softly shook me from my reverie. Moving to her workshop, I pushed the door closed and moved to the windows before calling Wendy.

Whispering, I gave her the bullet point version of what I'd learned. "Before I go any further, I need your help."

"What you need is to get out of there. We don't know for sure whether she's the killer, but if she is, she'll soon realize you're on to her."

"I've got Dickens with me, and I won't stay much longer. Just do this for me. It suddenly hit me that Emilia should be able to tell me whether Sophie left her flat Monday night and, if she did, whether she entered the spa."

Wendy blew out an exasperated breath. "You're just delaying, Leta. Unless Emilia was with her, how would she know?"

"It's the keypads at the spa. There are four altogether. Just tell her I need to know what activity was recorded that night. I should have thought of this earlier when I remembered my sister's system. She can check her app to see when the doors are locked and unlocked and when they open and close. She also has codes assigned to different people. Don't tell Emilia why. Just tell her she needs to call me ASAP."

I cracked the door in time to see Sophie tug the blanket over her shoulders. Rhubarb was tucked against her chest and meowed at the movement. Guilty or not, she was emotionally exhausted.

If the keypad data pointed toward her, there had to be somewhere she could be sequestered, preferably under lock and key, without alerting the Foxbournes. There was no telling how they would react to the news that Sophie could be the killer.

Just saying those words in my head gave me pause. She had means, motive, and opportunity, so why was I hesitant? I couldn't put my finger on it, but regardless, I needed to figure out where to put her.

I found myself wishing Gemma were here to take the problem off my hands, and before I could second-guess myself, I closed the door and called her.

Thankfully, she answered right away. "What did you think about the news from Jonas? He hasn't heard back from the Préfecture de Police yet, but I wouldn't be surprised if they have something on Edward too. Love 'em, leave 'em, and take a memento."

Not just a thief, but a thieving lothario. "I've been too busy to get to Jonas, but I'm not surprised. Was the memento a piece of jewelry, Gemma?"

"What? How on earth did you know that?"

"It's a long story, and it involves Sophie. I need your help."

As soon as I told her who Sophie's father was, she interrupted me. "Simon Green. That case was big. And Scotland Yard never learned who was supplying him with the stolen goods."

"Edward Foxbourne, for one, and you're not going to believe the rest of the story."

She interjected expletives as I shared Sophie's tale. By the time I was done explaining the blackmail and who the earrings belonged to, she was ready to hop in her car and attempt to reach us. But not before chastising me. "What part of no more digging did you not get, Leta Parker? I clearly told you to provide comfort and support and not another thing."

"That's why I need your help, Gemma. You know there's no way you can get here today. I can't believe it will, but if the keypad data points to Sophie, what then? Do I ask her if she killed Edward? And no matter what she says, what do I do with her? Am I right that she needs to be kept away from the others, regardless?"

Gemma was quicker than I was. "Hold your horses, Leta. You need to tread carefully, so for goodness' sake, do *not* ask her if she's the killer. Now, get Wendy over there so you're not alone with Sophie when she wakes up. Thankfully, you've already got the little hero dog with you. Have Wendy put Rob Thompson on standby. You'll need him regardless of which way this goes."

"Why Rob, and what if the keypad data clears her?"

"Rob because we don't want to involve the Foxbournes. No one's in the clear yet, but the family is higher on the suspect list than any of the hired help. And I understand Rob has the keys to everything, including the hunting lodge. We saw that place, and that's the best place to put Sophie. She needs to be sequestered for her own safety. If she's not the killer, she may know something that points to the killer, especially if she was upstairs the whole time. Something she's not aware of. Either way, we don't want her wandering around."

"And I'll wait until I get the keypad info before I do anything."

"Leta, you lost me."

"Sorry, Gemma. Way too much has happened this morning."

When I explained that Emilia was gathering data for me, Gemma's reaction surprised me. "Bloody hell, I can't believe I lost sight of the keypad. Good work, Leta. The records may or may not help, but it's better to avoid an embarrassing mistake. Can you imagine Viscount Foxbourne's reaction if you suggest his son's girlfriend is a murderer and you're wrong?"

As soon as she used St. John's title, I knew she was worried. "Gemma, the truth is I don't want it to be Sophie. But I don't have another plausible suspect at this point—emphasis on plausible."

She groaned. "Meaning you have all kinds of wild ideas, I'm sure. Would you care to enlighten me?"

I thought it was best not to apprise her of my guess about a motive for St. John. I was saved by the bell—a text from Emilia. She'd sent a photo of a bulleted list with a note that she wasn't sure how helpful it would be.

She had grouped each door with its times, rather than a timeline of comings and goings all night. That meant I had to check back and forth to get the entire timeline clear in my head. Paper and pencil would have been so much easier.

Front Entrance to Spa

- ☐ **6:34 PM** – Closed and locked
- ☐ **9:03 PM** – Unlocked and opened
- ☐ **9:04 PM** – Closed (not locked)
- ☐ **9:40 PM** – Opened and closed
- ☐ **9:54 PM** – Opened and closed
- ☐ **10:42 PM** – Opened
- ☐ **10:58 PM** – Closed
- ☐ **9:05 AM (Next Morning)** – Opened and closed

Back Entrance to Spa

- **6:38 PM** – Opened, closed, and locked

- **9:49 AM (Next Morning)** – Unlocked, opened, and locked

Back Entrance to Carriage House

- **6:39 PM** – Opened

- **6:42 PM** – Closed and locked

Sophie's Flat

- **6:43 PM** – Unlocked, opened, and locked

- **9:48 AM (Next Morning)** – Unlocked, opened, and locked

I breathed a sigh of relief when I saw that Sophie hadn't left her flat all evening. Unless she had shinnied down a drainpipe, she was in the clear. I also realized I had the time of death for Edward—between 10:42 and 10:58 p.m. What I didn't know was who had come and gone multiple times between 9:16 and 10:58 p.m.

Another text from Emilia popped up. "I thought it was strange the front door wasn't locked Wednesday morning until I remembered Uncle Edward's last-minute request for a massage. He often forgot to lock the door. It wouldn't have been the first time."

Emilia picked up right away when I called. "Was it helpful at all, Leta?"

"It's more than I knew before."

I wondered whether she realized that her uncle might still be alive if only he'd locked the door when he came in. "Sophie mentioned your father had a separate code. Was that the only different one?"

"Yes, and I honestly can't recall a time it's been used. Sophie, Uncle Edward, and I all used the same one—1608. Well, except for Sophie's flat. She has her own code for that. I'm glad you thought to ask." She cleared her throat. "Leta, we're all suspects, aren't we? Uncle Edward is dead, and someone I know, someone I'm related to, may have killed him. It's like some kind of awful Agatha Christie movie."

I didn't believe it, but I said it anyway. "We don't know, Emilia. It could be that something from your uncle's past caught up with him. Gemma's considering every angle, and we're helping as much as we can."

"I know, and no matter what, it's a comfort to Gran that you and Ellie and everyone else are helping. I'll let you go, Leta. I promised to help Bash. Thank you, for everything you're doing."

So much to think about. I forwarded Emilia's keypad text to Gemma with a note that Sophie was in the clear. Then I texted Wendy about Rob. Her response was that she was at the back door.

Sophie had budged only enough to snuggle deeper beneath the blanket, so I headed downstairs to let Wendy in.

It was déjà vu when I saw Ellie standing in the snow holding her shotgun. "Ellie, what on earth are you doing?"

"Wendy said you needed protection, so here I am. She's down the way calling Rob." Ellie pointed toward the other end of the carriage house. "Has Sophie confessed?"

Inviting her into the tiny foyer, I plopped down on the steps. "How much has Wendy told you?"

"Not enough. We were in a hurry. Ah, here she comes."

When Wendy arrived, she said Rob was on his way with the keys. "All I told him was that Gemma had requested his assistance, and we needed him to escort us to the hunting lodge and open it up. How much are you going to tell him?"

That was a good question. Ellie listened as Wendy and I debated what to reveal before deciding to be as brief as possible. We needed to tell him enough that he understood Sophie could be in danger and that his secrecy was of the utmost importance.

We heard him before we saw him. I'm not sure what I expected, but it wasn't an ATV. Of course, Foxbourne Park had ATVs. They had golf carts and horses. They probably had bicycles too. All that was lacking was a helicopter pad.

Doffing his cap, he approached us tentatively. "Pardon me, Lady Stow, but . . ."

Ellie glanced at her shotgun. "Don't worry, Rob, I know how to use it, but hopefully I won't have to."

If the circumstances weren't so serious, the exchange would have been amusing. I could imagine what was going through Rob's mind. "Rob, Gemma asked me to find a safe place for Sophie, somewhere no one will think to look for her. All I can tell you is that she may know something about Edward that puts her in danger. It may amount to nothing, but we can't take that chance. I must ask that you tell no one about this, neither the Foxbournes nor your family. Can I count on you?"

"That girl's like a second daughter to me. I'll do whatever I say. Shall I take her now?"

"Why don't you and Wendy prepare the lodge first. Get it warmed up, show Wendy where everything is, and come back for Sophie. I need to tell her the plan and pack up supplies for at least today and tonight."

Sophie wore a confused look as I attempted to explain what we were doing, but in the end, she acquiesced easily enough. The reality was that I was not only worried about her safety, but also that of the LOLs. We'd been involved in enough investigations to know that a killer could get antsy as questions were asked.

It was difficult to convey my concern. "Sophie, whoever killed Edward has to know you were up here that night. The more time that passes without the police arresting someone, the more worried the killer will grow. What if you heard something? What if you looked out your window and saw someone leaving the spa?"

"But I didn't, Leta. I was too busy."

"I believe you, Sophie, but the killer doesn't know that. You may have been completely absorbed in your work, but it's possible you heard or saw something you don't realize yet. And, honestly, I'm praying whoever it was doesn't worry too much about the questions we ladies have been asking. Did Bash tell you that his grandmother hired us?"

That question, at least, brought a small smile to her face. "Yes. He wasn't sure whether to be amused or grateful, but he trusts his gran." That was much the same reaction Emilia and St. John had expressed. Whatever. It served our purpose.

As she packed a set of warm clothes, I filled a grocery sack with coffee, tea, and snacks. Later, I'd pack a basket of leftovers to carry to her.

Downstairs, Ellie was sitting on the steps with her shotgun propped in the corner. "Hello, luv. You and I haven't been properly introduced. I'm Ellie, and I'll be spending the day with you."

Sophie gasped as she took in the shotgun. "Is that your gun?" She turned to me. "You weren't kidding, were you? You really are concerned for my safety."

"Yes, and you'll be in good hands. Be sure to get Ellie to tell you how she saved me from a pair of dognappers."

Dickens knocked into my knees. "That was a grand adventure. And it was snowy, just like it is now."

When we heard the motor, we met Rob outside. Ellie handed me the shotgun as Wendy hopped off. When the two women were settled, Ellie reached for her gun. "Leta, did you think it would bite you? The look on your face was priceless."

"Ellie, I've never held a gun in my life, much less a shotgun. The Dale Evans outfit I got one year for Christmas is as close as I've come." *And I'd like to keep it that way.*

CHAPTER SEVENTEEN

WE FOUND BELLE IN the dining room, sipping coffee and eating a cup of fresh fruit. "There you are. Edith said you'd gone for a walk, but we were beginning to think you'd gotten lost. And I've seen neither hide nor hair of Ellie."

She tilted her head toward the buffet on the far wall where Bash was lighting the cans of Sterno. "I was about to start the main course without you."

Wendy took the hint. "Mum, we'll tell you all about our walk over breakfast. It reminds me of *101 Dalmatians* with all the snow. Dickens and Lucky had a big time."

"Bash," I called as I walked toward the entry hall, "how's your family this morning?"

"Fair. Gran and Dad have already eaten, and now Dad's on calls. Emilia and Mum are glued to the telly for the latest weather news."

Charlotte was next on my list, but the first order of business was for me to call Jonas. Wendy had tried unsuccessfully, so we were still in the dark about the details of what he'd surfaced about Edward. With all that had been going on, Gemma and I never got beyond the love 'em and leave 'em part.

Jonas was delighted to hear my voice. "Leta, thank goodness. If I have to take one more call about someone stuck on the side of the road, I'll go barmy. I'd much rather talk about your latest case."

"You'd better not let Gemma hear you call it that, or she'll shoot both of us. Hopefully, whatever you've learned will add a missing piece to the puzzle, and she can wrap this case up soon. This storm isn't helping."

"I'm still waiting for a call from Paris, but the facts are pretty straightforward here. Your victim was accused of stealing jewelry from two different women in London—women he was in a relationship with. Gemma explained he was quite smart, and she thought these two were only the tip of the iceberg. Both were married to wealthy older men, and both accused Edward of stealing a valuable piece of jewelry."

"You used the word accused. Does that mean he wasn't arrested or convicted?"

"Exactly. It was a case of he said, she said. Neither woman wanted her husband to know, so both times, faced with the prospect of details getting out, the accusers withdrew their complaints."

What a perfect plan. Play paramour to women who couldn't risk being found out and be assured he could walk away with a memento he could easily turn into cash. I wondered how long the list of women was.

Jonas's news made it even more important to speak with Charlotte. Was she part of the love 'em, leave 'em, and take a memento pattern? Omitting that possible connection, I texted

Gemma my plan for the day. Interview Charlotte, followed by Annabelle and Rob—to document their comings and goings Tuesday night. I didn't honestly see the last two as suspects, but they needed to be checked off the list. She replied with a thumbs-up emoji.

Wendy and I left Belle in the drawing room to ponder the revelations we'd shared over breakfast, while we visited Charlotte. Dickens lay stretched out in front of the toasty fire, quite content to remain with Belle.

When we stuck our heads in the sitting room in the family wing, Charlotte waved us in as she muted the television. "This storm shows no sign of abating. They're saying there's another band of snow coming in."

That was a perfect segue to an account of my and Ellie's search for Dickens one snowy December. "We wound up spending the night in the inn that Gemma's parents own. Not quite as grand as this, but comfy and warm with plenty of food."

A faint smile crossed Charlotte's face. "Thankfully, the larder's full here as well, and the firewood is plentiful. If we lose power, poor Bash will have his work cut out for him keeping the fireplaces going." Her smile wavered. "Edward was a great help to him."

Wendy asked how she was bearing up and then explained that Gemma had asked us to learn as much about Edward as we could while she was stuck in Astonbury. "Every little detail builds a more complete picture of Edward and helps Gemma in her investigation."

I sat forward. "St. John said you and Edward got on well, perhaps better than the two of them did."

"Those two? Like oil and water. They were so different. Edward's lifestyle was anathema to St. John. Can you imagine St. John as a dilettante? That's how he described his brother. But the children adored Edward, and it was difficult to be in a low mood when he was around."

As she shared favorite memories of Edward, it was easy to see she cared for him. The question for me was, did it amount to anything more than the affection for a charming brother-in-law? "Tell me about his wife, Charlotte. St. John hinted that it was a marriage of convenience. Is that what you think?"

"What rubbish! St. John never could get beyond the years when Edward always had a beautiful young woman on his arm. I truly believe he and Marguerite loved each other, and he was completely devoted to her when she was ill that last year of her life. A good thing, too, because her children certainly weren't."

We carried on in this vein until I asked a question as though it had just occurred to me. "Charlotte, is there any chance you've misplaced your emerald earrings?"

She gave me a puzzled look. "What makes you think I've misplaced them?"

Shrugging, I fudged the truth with what I hoped was a believable explanation. "Maybe it was you wearing the gold ones that first night. I don't know exactly, and then . . . I found these." I pulled up the pictures on my phone.

"What on earth?" She murmured as she studied the photos. "Thank goodness, you found them. They were an anniversary gift from St. John, and I didn't know how I was going to tell him I'd lost them."

"When did you first notice they were missing?"

"Not until I looked for them Sunday. I haven't had an occasion to wear them since the holidays, and I knew St. John would expect me to show them off that first night. The choker was right where I always keep it, in the dresser drawer, but not the earrings. I was in a hurry, so I grabbed the gold ones, thinking I'd find the others when I looked harder. But I didn't. I looked all over our bedroom to no avail. And then, well—then Edward died."

Her eyes brimmed with tears. "It's so strange. Not long ago, he mentioned how lovely the earrings would look in a different design. It was just like Edward to sense I didn't care for them, when I've done such a good job of keeping that from St. John. I've never had the heart to tell him they weren't to my taste."

When she motioned toward my phone, I showed her the photos again. "Where . . . where did you find them?" She frowned. "Is that Emilia's spa?"

"Yes. Gemma and I found them there, in the massage room."

Her expression shifted from shocked to angry. "You mean Sophie had them? What was she doing with my earrings?"

"She didn't have them, Charlotte. Edward did."

She squinted. "Edward . . . not Sophie? Why?"

I didn't have to be a mind reader to sense what she was thinking. She'd jumped to the conclusion that Sophie had taken her earrings. And now, she was processing the reality that it was Edward. *Would she admit to herself that she'd misjudged her son's girlfriend?*

"He admired Sophie's talent, Charlotte. Based on what you've told me, is it possible he wanted her to draw a new design he could show you? A simpler one."

Her eyes glistened with tears. "That's the Edward that St. John never could appreciate. Maybe he *was* a dilettante, but he was a thoughtful one. He mentioned doing something like that for Marguerite's daughters, so they could share one of her necklaces."

I wondered whether there was any truth to the tale he'd spun about his wife's necklace. It didn't fit with his behavior toward Sophie, but a manipulative personality could easily be both threatening and thoughtful. Regardless, I didn't think it was a leap to conclude that there was nothing inappropriate in the relationship between Edward and Charlotte. And, if I was right, that not only eliminated Charlotte as a suspect, but St. John as well. Or at least, he didn't kill his brother over an affair. I couldn't rule out another motive popping up.

Next on the list was Annabelle.

CHAPTER EIGHTEEN

DICKENS AND BELLE WEREN'T in the sitting room, but they couldn't have gone far. We tracked them to the kitchen, where Dickens was happily chewing on a bone and Belle was sipping tea. "Girls, you've got to try Edith's ginger biscuits. They're perfect with tea."

I couldn't resist. "Ooh, they're like gingersnaps. You'll have to give me your recipe, Edith."

Swiping a stray strand of hair from her cheek, she smiled. "Let's trade. Your Greek salad recipe for my gingersnap one."

Belle laughed. "None of us at home even try, Edith. We just insist Leta make it for us on a regular basis." She nibbled another ginger biscuit. "Edith was about to tell me how she and Rob met. Did you know that she was a nurse?"

"Like you, Mum." Wendy turned to Edith. "And then you became a chef. What made you shift from nursing to cooking, Edith? Was it the hours?"

She stood with one hip propped against the counter. "Turned out there wasn't much of a shift because I never finished nursing school. Rob and I knew each other from church, and when he came to Foxbourne Park as a stable hand, we began to ride together. He helped Dad with the hunting events too. It was natural for an attraction to develop, and I was chuffed to bits when he started talking marriage. But I was in nursing school, and he didn't want to wait. It caused a bit of a kerfuffle, to be honest, and we went our separate ways. Except we both lived on the estate, and, well, we kept having brief encounters, if you catch my meaning."

"Sounds like a romance novel," said Wendy.

Edith blushed. "Well, it didn't seem romantic when I fell pregnant, but it all worked out in the end. And here we are, happily married all these years and with a beautiful daughter as a bonus."

Picturing Edith riding in her younger days, I wondered if she'd loved it as much as her daughter did now. "Do you still ride, Edith?"

"Gave it up when I was pregnant. I'd seen Edward thrown and wasn't going to chance it."

Wendy nodded. "That's right. You rode back for help that day. He was lucky you were there."

"We often got in a ride or two when he was home from school, and we sometimes packed a lunch. That day, I was folding the picnic blanket when he took off, and I've always wondered whether his horse was spooked by the blanket flapping in the breeze. Whatever did it, he took quite a fall."

She chewed her lower lip. "And not long after, I discovered I was pregnant. Those two things go together in my mind."

Leaving Edith to her cooking, we moved to the drawing room, where we brought Belle up to speed on the earrings. She tsked, tsked as she shook her head. "That Edward was quite a mix, wasn't he? If not for his threatening Sophie and stealing from his girlfriends, I could almost see him as likeable, even with the thievery."

I nearly choked. "Those are big ifs, Belle. If he hadn't been a jewel thief. If he hadn't threatened to ruin Sophie's life. Yes, he was thoughtful, and he was charming, but there's no escaping he was a scoundrel."

Pursing her lips, Wendy agreed. "And I nearly fell for it. Oh well, you're never too old to do something stupid."

Belle pointed to the pages taped to the wall. "I noticed we hadn't spoken with Edith. That's why Dickens and I visited the kitchen. The ginger biscuits were a bonus."

"Don't keep us in suspense, Mum. Did you learn anything beyond how Rob and Edith met?"

"Nothing helpful. It was easy to get her on the topic of Tuesday night, how she gave Leta bones for Dickens, took dinner to Annabelle's cottage, and returned to do a final tidying up. Said she'd be glad when the rest of the staff was back, that having Emilia and Bash underfoot wasn't the same as working with experienced kitchen help."

I chuckled. "I can only imagine. They want to help but are probably more in the way than anything else. Good catch on your part to speak with her, Belle. I think I assumed Gemma had covered that base before she left, but now we can add your info to our notes."

Wendy pecked Belle on the cheek. "Mum, we're off to talk to Annabelle. Can I get you anything before we leave?"

"No, luv. Believe it or not, I found a Josephine Tey book in the library. It's *The Daughter of Time*, one of her Inspector Grant mysteries. I always did like those books."

With Dickens in tow, Wendy and I traipsed in the direction of Annabelle's cottage. We crossed over the line of Edith's footsteps from the stables to the kitchen and then followed the trail left by Sophie. There were a handful of cottages scattered across the estate, but only one was occupied. Even without Sophie's footsteps, the smoke curling from its chimney would have made it easy to locate.

Annabelle was bringing in a load of firewood as we approached. With her hip to the front door, she invited us in. "You too, Dickens."

We made small talk while she added logs to the fire, but soon enough she gave us a questioning look. We'd decided Wendy would take the lead, so she began with an explanation of Gemma's absence and how she'd asked us to pitch in.

As agreed, I shared the why. "I know you're friends with Bash and Sophie. Has either of them mentioned the Little Old Ladies' Detective Agency to you? Or that Lady Lavinia also asked for our help?"

She gave me a bemused smile. "Yes, but I didn't take it too seriously. Sophie claims that one of you is nicknamed Miss Marple. Would that be the older white-haired lady? Sorry, the names are a muddle to me."

"Yes, and they call me Tuppence. But we're not the stuff of fiction." I made my explanation as brief as possible, sharing just enough to make our involvement believable. "Trust me, Gemma would rather be here herself, but she's relied on our help in the past, so we're doing what we can. She managed to notify everyone on the estate before she left yesterday, and next she would have documented everyone's movements for Tuesday evening.

That job's fallen to us, and we've already spoken with the family and Sophie and your mum. That leaves you and your dad."

Wendy leaned back on the sofa. "And after that, I plan to sit in front of the fire with my book and not budge for the rest of the day."

"Well, then, it sounds like a pot of tea is in order—or would you prefer cocoa?"

When we opted for cocoa, Annabelle busied herself in the kitchen. Wendy picked up after the steaming drinks were served. "Gemma also wants to know who visited the estate on Tuesday, so let's start with your riding schedule that day, Annabelle. I know you took Gemma out for a ride, and she enjoyed it immensely. Did you have any other customers Tuesday?"

She gave us the names of two regulars who rode Tuesday morning when Wendy was out with Edward. "Late afternoons bring the after-school crowd, but only two of the usual three made it. The last one called to say she had a cold."

Making a show of jotting notes, I watched attentively as Wendy shifted to later on Tuesday. "Now, how did you spend Tuesday evening?"

Annabelle attempted a smile. "Is this where I tell you what I watched on telly?"

"If it were me answering, it would be what book I read," I said.

"First, I hardly ever watch telly unless it's a program with Bash and Sophie. Tuesday night, I went to dinner with Edward. In Deddington."

So, it wasn't someone from the village he was out with!

"I think . . . I think that's why I was so shocked when Gemma told us. We'd had a lovely evening, and then . . ."

Dickens put his nose on her leg, and Wendy gave her a moment. "Did he drop you off here after dinner?"

"Yes. I opened a bottle of wine, and he stayed for a bit. He had an appointment with Sophie, but he kept delaying. He was trying to get my chin just right before he left, but I could tell his shoulder was giving him fits. That long ride with you did it in, Wendy. He knows better."

It was all I could do to keep mum until Wendy asked the obvious question. "Your chin? What was he doing to your chin?"

Annabelle chuckled. "He wasn't doing something *to it*. He was sketching it. Here, let me show you."

Retrieving a sketch pad from a shelf beneath the window, she handed it to Wendy. I moved to lean over Wendy's shoulder as she flipped through its contents. There were at least twenty sketches of Annabelle's head and neck. Some with her hair up. Some with it down. A few of her facing forward. Several with her giving a sideways or over the shoulder glance. And there it was—a page with the distinctive collar of a riding jacket sketched beneath her face.

Wendy seemed to be struggling for words, and I thought I knew why. She'd seen the painting on Edward's easel—the one of a woman on horseback. And she'd seen Annabelle's face in the sketchpad in the studio. Was this sketch pad an indication that Edward had made his decision?

I pointed to an image with the collar. "Annabelle, are you the model for Edward's latest project? The woman in the red riding jacket?"

Her mouth dropped open. "Yes, but how do you know about it?"

When I explained we'd visited the studio, she told us Edward had wanted to surprise her and that she hadn't seen it yet. "He wanted to do a portrait of me in return for my taking care of his horse, and me on horseback was the pose he was set on. I knew about his Lady Godiva era from Bash, so I jokingly told him I'd better be dressed in more than scarves. He assured me it would be tasteful and that he'd finish it before he left in March."

She flipped the page to another image. "We agreed that the ones with my hair up were quite appealing, though my real life updo runs more to a messy ponytail. Every time I turned around, he was taking a photo of me on horseback or sketching my face. Really, I didn't weigh in on much. All he asked was that I allow him to follow his creative process, and he promised he'd tweak anything I didn't care for."

Wendy finally found her voice. "Only Ellie and I have seen it, Annabelle, but we told Leta and my mum about it. It's quite tastefully done. It's a shame he didn't get to complete it."

Her eyes glistened with tears. "He was the sweetest man. I could talk to him about anything, and he never once tried to tell me what I *should* do—unlike my parents. They're all about *should* and *shouldn't*. You *should* settle down. You *should* marry James. You *shouldn't* spend time with Edward. Edward listened and helped me think things through. He was like the uncle I never had. I can understand why Bash and Emilia loved him so."

James? Where had I heard that name before? "Who is James?"

"My boyfriend." She didn't seem inclined to elaborate, but when neither I nor Wendy responded, she went on.

"He's a paramedic and works long hours. Mum thinks I don't make enough time for him and likes to remind me that I'm not getting any younger. As if marrying young like she did is the only way. She doesn't get that things aren't like that anymore."

"I went through that with my parents, too. When I finally married my first husband, they'd about given up on me." I felt a smile spread across my face. "That may be the first time I've used the phrase 'first husband' to refer to Henry. I'll have to get used to that." I explained that I'd been a widow when I met the man who would soon become my second husband.

It was time to get back on track. "Annabelle, can you take us through the rest of Tuesday evening. You said that Edward kept delaying his departure. What time did he finally leave?"

"That's easy. It was right before Mum showed up with leftovers. I'd already told her I was having dinner out, but she insisted on bringing them. I wish she hadn't, because we had a huge row. She ruined what had been an enjoyable evening. It's just as well Edward didn't come back. I'd have been horrible company."

Why would he come back so late? "Was he planning to return? After his massage?"

"Only to keep tweaking my chin. He felt he was close to being able to add my face to the painting, so I told him he could, but for no longer than an hour. The concept of an early night was foreign to him, but not to me."

I was sure Edward's lifestyle didn't lend itself to early nights or early mornings. "May I ask what you and your mother argued about?"

She pursed her lips. "I don't see that it has anything to do with Edward's death. It was our typical argument as of late. She was angry that I'd been out with Edward, not James. As if James was even available."

She broke off and shook herself. "It sounds odd when I put it that way. It's just that she had a bee in her bonnet about Edward and his conquests, as she called them. When Bash describes his uncle bringing home one beautiful woman after another, it's a funny family story. Mum sees it as some kind of character flaw."

"A character flaw?"

"A serial seducer is what she calls him."

I nearly spluttered. The image Edith painted for me was that of a charming scamp. She mentioned the women he brought home, but didn't malign him for his habit. Was she a consummate professional? An employee, nearly a member of the family, who would never say a negative word about the Foxbournes? Or was there something more to the dichotomy in her descriptions?

The wheels must have been turning in Wendy's head, as well. "Annabelle, I'm a bit thrown. If you saw Edward as a kindly uncle, why would your mum be concerned about you spending time with him? No matter his womanizing reputation, you two were more friends than anything else."

Annabelle rolled her eyes. "I know exactly why, and it was ridiculous. When I was a teenager and Edward dropped in and out, I was starstruck. If you think he's good-looking now, you should have seen him then. I guess you could say I mooned over him. But for goodness' sake, that was years ago."

How do I phrase this? "You mean your mother thought you had a thing for him?"

"Oh yes! And when she saw the sketch pad lying out Tuesday night, she was apoplectic." She stared into the distance before shaking her head. "I told her and Dad months ago that Edward was doing a portrait of me on horseback, so I don't know what set her off. Dad was chuffed about the idea. Mum didn't say much then, but lately she's been fixated on the nudes he painted years ago. I don't understand it. His work included so much more than that. Like his painting of Mum, the one that hangs in the kitchen."

Wendy voiced what I was thinking. "Annabelle, you may have viewed Edward as an uncle, but is it possible that he saw your relationship as something more? The cozy evenings, the dinners out. Did you ever wonder if he was attracted to you?"

When her eyes darted about, I knew I had my answer. Finally, she cleared her throat. "A few times, but I didn't encourage him. If not for James, I might have. But I love James. I was even thinking I might give him the painting if it turned out well."

I was willing to bet that Edith saw it differently—that she read Edward's intentions and thought it was only a matter of time.

After a loaded silence, Annabelle added, "Edward and I had an easy, comfortable relationship that mum never understood. Let's leave it at that."

It was time to bring things to a close. "Sounds like you had quite a roller-coaster evening."

"That's one way to describe it. Thankfully, Mum didn't stay. She left in a huff, muttering, 'Wait 'til I tell your father.' As though I were a five-year-old. And that was the end of my evening. When Edward didn't show up, I assumed he'd decided to call it a night, and I'd see him in the morning at the stables."

When I gave Wendy a 'now what' look, she stood. "Just one more thing, Annabelle. Did you by chance call James after your mum left?"

"No, but he called me later when his shift ended, and he got an earful. Turnabout's fair play. I hear often enough about his mum and dad."

She gave Wendy a curious look. "Guess it's like a mystery book. We all need an alibi, don't we?"

When her phone emitted a horse whinny, she chuckled and picked up. "Speak of the devil. I was just saying you might need an alibi. Hold on. I was just messing about. No, it's not the police."

She covered the phone with her hand. "James doesn't really need an alibi, does he?"

Before we could respond, she went back to James. "Don't worry. I'll be sure to tell them. Let me finish up here, and I'll call you back."

She bit her lip. "It's easy to joke about an alibi, because I know he has one. You can't be on shift in an ambulance without people knowing where you are."

As often happened, Wendy and I were sync and said, "True," at the same time. Who knows why? I made a mental note that we should at least consider asking Gemma to check.

As Dickens pranced ahead of us, Wendy and I attempted to process what we'd heard and to determine which points were pertinent versus simply surprising. It was Annabelle who Edward took to dinner Tuesday night. She had a boyfriend. She wasn't Edward's lover, though he may have hoped she would be. Edith disapproved of her relationship with him. Edward had settled on Annabelle as the face for the painting. It was a lot to take in.

As Dickens came running with a stick, I stopped. "Wendy, it's time we had a powwow. We may be down one little old lady, but you, me, and your mum need to make sense of all this. I feel as though the answer is staring us in the face."

CHAPTER NINETEEN

THE DRAWING ROOM WAS nice and toasty, and we weren't surprised to find Belle had dozed off. As soon as Dickens bounded in and put his paw on her knee, she yawned. "Hello there. Did you have a good walk?" She looked over her shoulder at us. "And did you two have a productive talk with Annabelle?"

Shedding my coat, I moved to the flip chart. "I'll say. Productive, surprising, shocking. I'm still trying to digest it. Let's capture what she told us, and then I think we need to develop a timeline with all the moving parts or people."

As soon as I wrote the name James, it hit me. "I knew his name sounded familiar. Edith was on the phone with Annabelle when I went to the kitchen Tuesday night, and the conversation makes sense now. She said something like, 'you mean you're not with James? You're with him?' and it went downhill from there. *Him* had to be Edward. She was furious that Annabelle was having dinner with Edward."

Belle studied the page. "It's one thing not to want your daughter to date an older man, but Annabelle's a grown woman. If she didn't live near her parents, if she lived in London, she'd see who she pleased. And if she made a mistake, she'd figure it out soon enough."

She gave Wendy a knowing look. "It's not like I wanted Wendy to marry a Yank and move overseas, but she'd made up her mind. It wasn't my place to stand in her way."

"And you know, Mum, I don't regret it. I might never have left England if not for getting married. I enjoyed those years teaching in Charlotte, even if the marriage didn't last."

Wendy grabbed a marker and tore a page from the pad. "Let's start the timeline with Edward leaving Annabelle's cottage. We don't know where every single person was, but we know when the spa door opened and closed. And we think we know the time of Edward's death. Give me the timing, Leta."

Pulling out my phone, I found Emilia's text and scanned it.

Front Entrance to Spa

- **6:34 PM** – Closed and locked

- **9:03 PM** – Unlocked and opened

- **9:04 PM** – Closed (not locked)

- **9:40 PM** – Opened and closed

- **9:54 PM** – Opened and closed

- **10:42 PM** – Opened

- **10:58 PM** – Closed

"It must have been Edward who came in around nine. Either he stepped out or someone else arrived forty minutes later, and around fifteen minutes after that—someone came or went. If it was someone who came in, I see the person staying and having a brief discussion with Edward before leaving. What do you think?"

Wendy stood back from the timeline. "It doesn't make sense that Edward left. He had probably disrobed and stretched out on the massage table by then, so I agree with you. Edward arrived, and someone else came in and conversed with him for ten minutes before departing. Give me the rest of it."

"Let me see. All of that occurred before ten. Again, when you consider that Edward was undressed, that means it was someone else who opened the door at 10:42, stayed fifteen minutes or so and left. That has to be when Edward was stabbed, because that's the last activity until Emilia opened the door the next morning. We know it wasn't Sophie because she didn't exit her flat at all."

Belle spoke up. "When did Edith get to Annabelle's cottage?"

"Hold on, Mum. I can come up with an approximate time." Wendy scribbled 9ish for Edith's arrival. "She arrived right after Edward left. And I doubt their row lasted long, so I'd say she left around 9:15."

The corners of Belle's mouth twitched up. "And her parting comment was that age-old admonishment, 'Wait until I tell your father.' Some things never change."

"Sounds like she went straight home to vent. We need to ask Rob what time she got to the stables that night," I said.

Jotting that question on the timeline, Wendy squinted. "Except, Mum, didn't she tell you she came back to the kitchen to finish tidying up? It was bones for Dickens, food to Annabelle, and back to the kitchen."

"Yes, but I suppose she could have done both—returned to tidy up, as she said, and then gone home. What's important is the time she finally arrived home. As long as it was by 10:30 or so, that would put her in the clear, right?"

Thinking aloud, I played out the scenario. "Unless she went back out. Or what if she went to tidy up, like she told you, Belle? And she fumed and went to the spa to give Edward a piece of her mind before ten. Could she have been angry enough to kill him, dash out in a panic, and go back to clean up when she got her wits about her?"

"Am I the only one who thinks it strange the way she talks about Edward?" said Wendy. "With us, she reminisces fondly about his escapades. But with Annabelle, she bad-mouths him. She's the poster child for speaking out of both sides of your mouth."

"That's exactly what I thought when I heard the words serial seducer. Add that to how irate she was on the phone with Annabelle and again that night at the cottage, and it's possible . . ."

Wendy finished my sentence. "Possible that she's our killer. All the more reason we need to speak with Rob."

We were mulling that over when Ellie called. "Hello, Leta. How are things progressing?"

Putting her on speakerphone, I did my best to share our findings.

She wasn't surprised about what we'd learned from Annabelle. "Yes, Sophie's shared as much. It was extremely uncomfortable for her that Emilia, Bash, and Annabelle saw Edward as a kindly uncle. The poor girl had no one she could turn to. She's also well aware that Edith's been a broken record about Edward to Annabelle."

When we told her how we'd landed on Edith as a plausible suspect, there was a long silence on her end. "Sorry, ladies. I had to think that through. Before you get stuck on that idea about Edith, I suggest you speak with Lavinia. Tell her you need to know more about Edward as background. It won't be difficult to get her talking. Peel back the onion on everything you can. My sense is there's more we need to know about his paintings, his friendship with Edith, and his relationship with St. John. And let's not forget Rob. We know little or nothing about him."

Belle nodded in agreement. "Good catch about Rob, Ellie. After all, Gemma did say it takes some strength to stab a man in the back. You didn't mention Charlotte—do you think we've learned all we need to about her connection with Edward?"

"Yes, what she told Leta about the earring situation was quite believable, even comforting. I found myself wanting to believe Edward took them so he could surprise her with a new setting. I'd hate to think he was a total rotter. Let Lavinia talk. She's bound to touch on how he and Charlotte got on once you get her going."

We decided it didn't take all three of us to speak with Lavinia, and Wendy suggested that Belle and I handle that interview.

"Shall I leave Dickens with you, Wendy?"

"Sure. What's going on in this case has sparked an idea for my book, and I want to capture it before it disappears. Dickens can be my footrest while I jot it down."

He barked and stretched out by her feet. "I'm the best-ever footrest as long as you rub my belly."

She had no idea what he'd said, but that didn't stop her from propping her feet on him. "You'd think he understood me. You're a sweet boy, Dickens."

When Bash called my name, Belle and I stopped by the front desk. "Leta, how was Sophie when you spoke with her this morning? I'm worried about her."

Uh-oh. What had Sophie told him? "She was fine, Bash. What's got you worried?"

He blushed. "I thought she'd want company, but she asked me to leave her be to focus on her jewelry."

"I suspect that's a good distraction for her. If it were me, I'd dive into a book, but each to his own."

"You're probably right, Leta. It's me who wants company, but I've got plenty of work to keep me busy."

As Belle and I rode the elevator up, she complimented Sophie. "That was quick thinking on her part. She had an awful morning, but she didn't give anything away."

Lavinia was in the family sitting room reading. "You two are a sight for sore eyes. I keep reading the same line over and over because I can't stop thinking about Edward. Where's Ellie? Do you know anything yet?"

Taking a seat in a chair with an ottoman, Belle shook her head. "Nothing to share yet, but we could use your help. Would you mind talking to us about Edward? We need to know him better so we can ask the right questions. Leta has her fiancé doing online research to learn more about his artwork and his life in France, but you're the best person to bring him to life for us."

I chose an overstuffed chair and curled my legs beneath me. "In other words, we need a fuller picture of him. I spoke briefly with St. John, and as you can imagine, he was focused more on Edward's scrapes than anything else. To Emilia and Bash, he's their lovable uncle who married a countess and happened to be an artist. We want to know the man beneath that surface. We're hoping you can tell us about the real Edward."

Lavinia carefully placed her bookmark between the pages of her book. "I'd like nothing better than to reminisce about Edward. A mother has a completely different view of her son than other family members do. Much as Edward had a slanted view of St. John as a stuffy, serious bore, St. John saw his younger brother only as an irresponsible wastrel. Irresponsible he may have been, but there was such joy in Edward."

As she closed her eyes, a faint smile appeared on her face. "I'm sure you want to hear about his adult life, but will you indulge me? May I start with his childhood?"

At my encouraging nod, she began by describing him as a cherubic baby. "We tried for years to have another child after St. John, and Edward's arrival ten years later was a surprise, but a joyous one. Not to St. John, of course. Edward was just a bother to him."

Her entertaining anecdotes painted a picture of an idyllic childhood. With St. John off at school, Edward had added a new chapter to his parents' lives. There was nothing he wouldn't try, whether it was climbing trees, digging for treasure by the gazebo, or diving in the pond in search of the Loch Ness monster. The soul of adventure was how she described him. "His father was fit to be tied when he drew on his bedroom wall at around age six. It was his first foray into art, and he never stopped. I mean, he stopped drawing on the walls, but he filled sketch pads with birds and squirrels and horses."

And it was clear he had never stopped. "Was he a solitary child, Lavinia? I imagine that living on a large estate, he didn't encounter many other children."

"That's true, but when Edith came along two years later, they became bosom buddies. She may have been St. John's shadow when he was home from school, but it was she and Edward who palled around the rest of the time. When he crafted wooden swords and shields, she joined in the fun. Edith was never the damsel in distress. She was right beside him playing in the mud and climbing into the tree house. When they took to riding, that was it. They were inseparable."

I thought about how different schooling was in the UK versus the States. "How old was Edward when he started school? He must have made other friends there."

"He did. When he went to prep school, he got along with everyone, and he brought various and sundry friends home. Typical of boys that age, they wanted nothing to do with Edith. Girls were inferior creatures to them."

"But it was only a few years until they looked at girls differently, wasn't it?"

My question elicited a chuckle. "But of course. There were quite a few tongue-tied young men whenever Edith came into view. When you look at Annabelle, you can see why. Edward was right when he said she was the spitting image of her mum."

Belle smiled. "Puts me in mind of my Peter and his friends, except they were mad for bicycles. They wouldn't bother with girls other than Wendy until they were older. And at best, they tolerated her."

I pictured Peter with his girlfriend Lucy. He hadn't had a girl-friend to speak of until he was in his mid-fifties, and it looked like Lucy might be a keeper. "Lavinia, I've heard about the beautiful women Edward brought home later in life, but what about when he was in prep school and at uni?"

"He was so unlike St. John in that regard. St. John had a few girlfriends, but when he met Charlotte straight out of uni, that was it. Love at first sight. Edward, on the other hand, had a bevy of beauties, as his father used to say. When we visited him at uni, he had a new girl on his arm every time. What would they call him these days? A chick magnet?"

Seeing how easily he'd charmed Wendy, I could believe it. "Did he bring any of them home? I know it was later in life that he married, but surely he had a serious girlfriend before then."

"If he did, he kept it quiet. The first time he brought a girl home was after he graduated and moved to France. And after that, it was a new one every time. If you want to see the history of Edward's love life, you can find it in his Lady Godiva series. He must have painted twenty different women in that pose."

The canvases leapt to mind, but I hadn't realized there were so many. "Lavinia, what attracted him to France? Was living abroad a longtime goal of his?"

"I don't think Edward ever had a longtime goal. It was when he was recovering from shoulder surgery the summer before his senior year that he became fixated on France. Something about his arm hanging useless by his side must have made an impact. I remember the surgeon coming to the waiting room to say it was taking much longer than he'd expected because Edward's shoulder was hanging on by a thread. He's never seen one so badly torn."

Belle's nursing background kicked in. "That can be a painful injury and a lengthy recovery. What can you tell us about his riding accident? I understand Edith was with him."

"It was a blessing she was home from nursing school, and that they rode together most days. I think she was frightened half to death, not knowing at first how badly he was hurt when his horse threw him, whether he'd hit his head, broken his arm, or exactly what was going on.

"She had to leave him and ride to the stables to get Rob. He rushed out with one of those quad bikes we used for tending the grounds and loaded Edward onto a trailer attached to the back. I can only imagine what he went through—unable to remount his horse, doubled over in pain, and having to endure that rough, jolting ride. It must've been agony for him, every bump in the path jarring his poor shoulder. I wasn't there, of course, but Edith and Rob painted a pretty vivid picture."

I clutched my arm. "It hurts just to hear you describe it. I guess that was the end of his riding that summer."

Looking into the distance, Lavinia shook herself. "It was the end of many things. Edward never came home for an extended stay after that, and his new catchphrase became 'life is short.' He'd always been fun-loving and adventurous, but now he was all about living life to its fullest. For all intents and purposes, it was also the end of his and Edith's childhood friendship. They never rode together again and that fall, she married Rob. They'd been going out for a while, but when Edward came home that summer, they broke up. I don't know that Edward had anything to do with that, but I'm sure Rob was glad to see the end of him.

"When I think of that summer, I hear the quote, 'To every-thing there is a season, and a time to every purpose under the heaven.' I see it as the last idyllic summer for both Edward and Edith. By the next summer, Edith had given up nursing school and had a newborn. Edward had graduated from uni and was part of a studio collective in Montmarte, where he waited tables and shared a flat with fellow starving artists. They were adults with adult responsibilities."

To me, it sounded as though Edward was still living a carefree life. Being a starving artist likely fit with his vision of living life to the fullest. I imagined him painting and bedding beautiful models, drinking red wine, and strolling along the Seine. He took on the persona of a starving artist, but he wasn't penniless. He didn't have to live off of his art because he had an allowance from his father. It was only Edith who had true adult responsibilities.

Lavinia may have thought her son was starving, but it was highly unlikely. "Did you worry about him, Lavinia? Were you hoping he'd get a real job like St. John?"

"Goodness no. St. John's world wasn't for Edward. He'd have been miserable. Edward eventually began to show his work in galleries and earn a modest income. He had a charming flat that doubled as his studio and attracted a few wealthy patrons. Meeting Marguerite, however, changed everything—for a time, at least."

"Why only for a time? Because she died?"

"No, not that. Her connections opened doors for him in all the right circles, elevating his name and reputation. But after they married, his focus shifted. I think he became enamored with their lavish lifestyle and let his art fall by the wayside. When she died, he returned to painting, but by then, he was nearly starting from scratch. The art world can be unforgiving. Out of sight, out of mind."

The prodigal son returns. "Is that what brought him home? Did he need a respite or a fresh start?"

With a sigh, she rolled her eyes. "I could pretend he missed us, but I know better—St. John made sure of that. Edward had burned through whatever money Marguerite left him, and let's just say a few of his . . . associations with married women didn't end well."

That told me St. John hadn't shared the messy "he said, she said" details I'd learned of from Jonas. Lavinia had no idea her son was more than just a down-at-the-heels artist—that he was, in fact, a jewel thief. I couldn't help but wonder how much St. John knew. Had he put two and two together? He likely knew about the accusations, as did Gemma, but not the whole truth. It was Sophie's revelations that tied it all together.

Belle shifted gears with her next question. "Lavinia, what did Charlotte think of Edward? Was she in St. John's camp or was she more forgiving of his foibles?"

"They got on quite well. In the beginning, what she knew of Edward came from St. John because their paths crossed so infrequently. Charlotte and St. John were either in London or traveling on business, and Edward was at uni and then in France. So, yes, in those early years, she looked askance at Edward. But when he married Marguerite and we saw more of him, Charlotte got to know and like them both. She and I enjoyed Edward's fun-loving side, the part that drove St. John crazy."

Lavinia chuckled. "Even St. John had to admit that Edward was an asset during high season. He charmed the guests, and he was a hit as a tour guide or a fourth at bridge. As far as I could tell,

Edward enjoyed himself too. And, of course, Bash and Emilia adored him. I began to hope he'd stay long-term, but I knew in my heart that would never happen. Still, if I had to lose him, I'm grateful I got to have him at home this past year."

On that bittersweet note, Belle and I said our goodbyes. Lavinia seemed at peace, at least for the moment, though the grieving process for her was far from over.

As we boarded the elevator, Belle was quiet until we started our descent, and then completely floored me.

CHAPTER TWENTY

"Edith was in love with Edward." A satisfied smile appeared on Belle's face.

"What?"

"Think about it, Leta. That explains her over-the-top reaction to Annabelle spending time with him. And given Edward's track record, I'm willing to bet that they slept together that summer. The picnics when they went riding? It fits. Whether Edward loved her or not, he wouldn't have thought twice about it."

I knew she was right. "And she certainly didn't want her daughter doing the same. She had to be horrified at the thought, but she couldn't tell Annabelle why."

Belle made a choking sound. "I can't imagine telling Wendy that I'd slept with someone she was seeing. The idea makes me want to gag."

When we reached the drawing room, the words tumbled out. "Wendy, your mum is brilliant."

Wendy's mouth dropped open as Belle shared her lightbulb moment. "It made perfect sense when I heard Lavinia describe

Edward and Edith's history. Except that in a Hallmark movie, they would have married and lived happily ever after—the viscount's son and the game warden's daughter."

"Mum, do you think that means Edith killed him?" She scrunched her mouth to the side and squinted. "Nah. As embarrassing as it was, she would have told the truth to Annabelle before she did that . . . wouldn't she?"

I was asking myself the same question. "That's more believable than Edith killing her childhood friend."

Hopping to her feet, Wendy grabbed her coat. "I'd have to agree, but we'll know for sure once we visit Rob. I see us checking her off the list once he tells us what time she got home Tuesday night."

"Belle, are you okay if we take Dickens with us? He'd enjoy visiting the horses."

"No worries, luv, but when you get back, I say we have lunch."

Dickens gave a happy bark. "Don't forget the carrots."

When we returned from fetching the carrots, Bash rushed to open the front door for us. "The wind is picking up again, ladies. Are you sure you're dressed warmly enough? I have extra scarves and gloves behind the desk if you need something more."

"What we need," said Wendy, "are snowshoes, but we'll manage. My fashionable fleece-lined suede boots are probably done for, but that's okay. It's an excuse to buy a new pair."

Dickens darted off as Bash closed the door behind us. A dark flash appeared in the distance, and I thought it was a fox frolicking in the snow until Dickens barked, "It's Lucky," and took off.

As we entered the stables, we heard the steady scrape of a pitchfork mingled with the occasional nicker of horses. Annabelle and Rob were working in tandem. She forked up the soiled straw and heaved it into a wheelbarrow, and her father came behind her to toss in handfuls of fresh hay and layer it across the floor.

Annabelle spied us first and must have noticed the carrots. "Come to feed the horses? You'll want to start at the far end where everything's clean. And you know the puppies are down there, too. They're sound asleep again."

Wiping his brow, Rob joined us at the first stall. "Ladies, if you need me, you'll let me know, right?"

I answered his unspoken question. "Sophie's fine, Rob, but we need a quick word with you after we've handed out all the carrots."

"Anything I can do to help. Just say the word."

It was easy to imagine all was right with the world as I communed with the horses, but I knew I was delaying the inevitable.

Dickens came running and skidded to a stop beside me. "We saw a fox. I've never seen one before. I can't wait to tell Christie."

Ruffling his cold fur, I whispered, "You'll have to tell her when we call home later."

When Lucky ran up behind him, the two sprinted toward the puppy stall, and I knew he'd be fully occupied for the next little while.

In the office, Rob poured tea before leaning back in his chair. "I figured you'd get around to me sooner or later. You've interviewed my wife and daughter, so that only leaves me."

Once again, Wendy took the lead. "You're right. Gemma's directing from afar, and once we've got your statement, we'll be done with our assignments."

"Other than ensuring Sophie is safe, that is." I leaned forward. "You don't know how much we appreciated your help this morning."

He tut-tutted and let Wendy proceed. "It's just like the BBC mysteries, Rob. We need to know what you did Tuesday evening. I imagine you have a routine."

"Aye. We don't have many riders right now, but we've got the same number of horses. And they all need tending to." For a moment, he gazed at Wendy as though he wasn't seeing her. "Sorry, I was thinking of Edward. I keep expecting to see him first thing every morning. For as long as I've known him, he's been keen on his dawn rides. And this winter, he's also pitched in currying the horses."

That was a good opening for Wendy. "How long have you known him, Rob? Did you grow up on the estate, like Edith?"

"Not quite. I took an after-school job helping her dad with whatever needed doing, and once I was done with school, he hired me full-time to tend to the stables. Still lived at home with my mum and dad. Didn't move here until I married Edith."

"And that's when you got to know Edward?"

"In the summers, yes. He was off at school the rest of the time. And after he moved to France, we didn't see much of him." A smile crept across his face. "When he visited with his wife, he still took his morning rides, and the two of them rode together in the afternoons. She was a good horsewoman."

He shook himself. "But you asked about my routine. With no guests this winter, Annabelle and I can tend to the horses earlier in the evenings, and then I take myself to my easy chair. Until you arrived on Sunday, her mum and I had a few weeks of eating dinner together at a reasonable hour, watching telly, and turning in at our usual time. Cooking dinner for the family doesn't keep her as busy as feeding guests. All in all, it's been nice having a bit of a break."

Wendy and I exclaimed over Edith's cooking before Wendy continued with her questions. "Can you lay out the evening in detail for me, Rob? Did you go anywhere other than upstairs after you were finished with your day's work?"

"Nope. When I'm done, all I want is my supper and my slippers. With Edith up at the main house, I heated my meal and watched telly. I knew she'd bring us a plate, but it would be too late for eating by then. Most nights, I eat the meal from the night before. Tuesday night it was the lamb and potatoes from Monday. Nice and hearty."

"What time did Edith get home?"

"Let me think. It was after nine when she called to tell me she'd stopped by Annabelle's but was going back to the main house to do a few more things. She made noises about her routine being off after a month tending only to the family."

"That's a long day," Wendy said. "What time was it when she finally made it home?"

He rubbed his forehead. "You know, I'm not sure. I climbed in bed at ten and didn't hear her come in. She's not usually that late, but it's all on her right now with the regular help not back yet. When we're fully staffed, she's usually here by nine, ready to put her feet up."

So much for Edith having an alibi. I could only hope my thoughts weren't visible on my face.

Wendy asked a few innocuous questions about Rob's morning routine before wrapping up with a question about the forecast.

Rob waved his hand toward the office window. "Doesn't look good, ladies. They're expecting another band of snow by late afternoon. Edith tells me Bash is trying to get her to put on a pot of soup and call it a day after tea. But if I know my wife, she'll stay through dinner."

Wendy and I made a big deal out of throwing snowballs for Dickens and Lucky as we walked toward the manor house. When I judged we were far enough from the stables, I turned toward her. "What next? I say call Gemma and batten down the hatches. Sophie should be safe with Ellie and her shotgun, and no matter whether it's Edith or someone else, our killer isn't going anywhere."

"Get real, Leta. It has to be Edith. Go down the list. Means, motive, and opportunity. Who else can it be?"

"I admit she has it all, but the SOCOs and Gemma mentioned needing the strength to thrust that knife in and do the job with only one blow. I'm just trying to cover all the bases. What if St. John has a strong motive we're unaware of? It's more likely he had the strength to do it."

"It's the knowledge of anatomy and lack of an alibi that seals the deal for me. Edith went to nursing school. St. John may have strength going for him, but Edith knew exactly where to plunge the knife." She tossed another snowball. "What will it take to convince you?"

I blew out my breath. "It's just difficult to imagine that her conversation with Annabelle set her off enough to kill Edward. Confront him, maybe, but kill him? I can see her storming into the spa straight from Annabelle's cottage and telling him off, but who went in after ten?"

Wendy veered off toward the carriage house. "Bear with me. Think of this as one of our cozy mysteries. Our sleuths would have done a more thorough search of Edward's studio, and I think we should too. Besides, you haven't seen the painting of Annabelle."

Whatever she had in mind, it couldn't hurt to let her follow her nose. Upstairs in the studio, she stood in the middle of the room while I strode to the easel and removed the cloth. It was a striking image. The fitted red jacket with brass buttons had a black velvet standup collar, and the shoulders were lightly padded, giving it a feminine touch. With the blouse unbuttoned, the image was elegant yet provocative.

"I'm glad Ellie thought to remove the cloth. This is amazing."

When Wendy didn't respond, I turned around. Leaning over an ancient wooden file cabinet, she was thumbing through a file folder. "Wendy, what are you looking at?"

She motioned me over. "This folder was sitting on top of the cabinet. Look inside. Edward may still have been working to perfect Annabelle's chin, but he did several trial sketches of the entire painting using different versions of her face—with her hair up, with it down, some facing front, several in profile."

As I flipped through the sketches, Wendy turned toward the easel. "I don't think these have anything to do with Edward's death, but seeing them makes me think back to Edith blowing up at Annabelle."

"And?"

"What if Edith also saw the painting? It wouldn't have taken much for her to put two and two together—to realize what Edward had in mind. It's not Lady Godiva, but it's . . ."

"Suggestive. But Edith didn't see it, so what difference does it make?"

Wendy moved to the easel. "Let's imagine that she did. And she saw it as confirmation of her suspicions, that he was intent on bedding her daughter. This was the lead-up, the prelude."

Imitating a Hollywood gunman, she pantomimed firing a pistol and putting it to her mouth to blow on it. "And for Edith, it was the trigger."

"A tad dramatic, but I get the point. And she went downstairs and confronted him."

I tried to picture the scene. "Except, wouldn't he have sat up if she was yelling at him? Can you see him just lying there on his stomach while she accosted him?"

Wendy played it out. "He's lying on the table. Maybe he dozed off while he was thinking Sophie would show up eventually. Edith walks in, sees him, and lays into him. He wakes up, raises his elbows, turns over, and yes, he sits up. What makes him lie back down?"

"The only thing that makes sense to me is that she stormed out after saying her piece, and he rolled back over. Unless he did that while she was still yelling at him. Maybe in an attempt to indicate the conversation was over. And then what? The snub incenses her, and she grabs a dagger, and stabs him in the back? If that's what happened, why did she come back?"

Staring at the easel, Wendy snapped her fingers. "To wipe the handle of the knife clean. Because it wasn't malice aforethought. She stabbed him in a fury, calmed down, and realized she had to cover her tracks. That's it. We've solved the case."

CHAPTER TWENTY-ONE

As we stepped into the cold and pulled the door to, I noticed something I'd missed before. There was a keypad on the exterior wall. I recalled Bash mentioning that he had the code, but that Edward rarely locked the door. Regardless, there should be a record somewhere of the comings and goings.

We weren't ready to run into Edith, so we climbed the front steps with Dickens at our heels. I was in luck—Bash was manning the front desk. In a hurried whisper, I asked Wendy to follow me.

When I asked about the keypad, he pulled up an app on his phone. "It's all right here. Let me see. If you're looking at Tuesday, no one went in or out all day. It wasn't until 9:59 that the door opened and closed. And then again at 10:15. You know, Uncle Edward often spent most of the night painting. Some idea would strike him, and off he'd go." Suddenly, he blanched. "Was that what he did before he died that night?"

Because of the questions we'd asked, Sophie and Emilia had an idea of the time of death, but no one else in the family knew anything more specific than Tuesday night. "I can't say Bash, but one more thing. Can you pull up the times for the kitchen door that night?"

As he showed me the data, an idea took shape—one that might better explain the sequence of events. The look on Wendy's face told me she was thinking the same thing.

We were careful not to say a word until we closed the door to the drawing room. "Belle, it's hard to say who's the better detective, you or your daughter. You've both been brilliant today."

"Don't keep me in suspense. I've been sitting here wondering whether it could really have been Edith. I've even started considering Rob as a jealous husband or an overprotective father."

Wendy and I tag-teamed on what we'd learned at the stables and in Edward's studio. I glanced at my notes and laid out the timing. "Belle, we know Edith got home after ten, and now we also know that someone visited Edward's studio Tuesday night—and that the kitchen door was closed and locked at 9:55. When you add the spa door data, I think we have a plausible scenario." I jotted the sequence of events on a clean page.

- Edith confronts Edward & leaves the spa

- She fumes in the kitchen

- She discovers the painting in the studio

- Edith kills Edward

"Great minds *do* think alike. What do you say, Mum?"

Belle held up her hand. "Let me think. Edith is angry when she leaves Annabelle's. She and Edward have it out and she leaves the spa. Who knows what he said to her, but she's even angrier. I can imagine her returning to the kitchen, slamming things around, and having a brainstorm. Maybe Edward tells her she's making a big deal over nothing, and Edith wants to see what she can find in the studio. She discovers the painting. It may not be a Lady Godiva image, but she's sure he has seduction in mind."

She looked at Wendy. "How am I doing?"

I answered before Wendy could. "Pretty darned good, Miss Marple. What we don't know is what she was thinking. She returns to the spa and stabs him. Did she walk in intent upon killing him, or did seeing him asleep trigger the idea? He had to be asleep, or he would have fought back. But he never had a chance."

Wendy stood with her arms akimbo. "I say it's time to call Gemma and tell her we've cracked the case."

Snapping a photo of the timeline, I texted it to Gemma with Wendy's comment. "Any bets on how long it takes her to call me?"

Our chuckles were cut short when my phone rang. "Leta, there must be more to the story. Good work finding the data on the doors, but how do you know it was Edith going in and out of them?"

I shifted the phone to speaker mode and suggested Wendy lead off with what Charlotte had to say. Gemma had the same reaction I'd had to Charlotte's assumption that it was Sophie who had her earrings. "Such an uppity response. To leap to the conclusion it had to be the hired help."

After asking a few clarifying questions, she complimented us on eliminating a suspect. "Removing another family member from the list will make the powers that be happy. I had enough interaction with Emilia and Bash to be convinced neither of them were responsible. The same for Lavinia, but St. John and Charlotte were more buttoned up. St. John wasn't on your to-do list for today. Should I assume you've scratched him off too?"

"I did wonder about him," I said, "because it seemed believable that Edward and Charlotte could have had a thing. But once we ruled that out, well, motive was an issue."

"And it's not for Edith? I'm dying to hear how you landed on her."

Wendy started with our trek to Annabelle's cottage. "Remember what Ellie and I discovered in Edward's studio? And that we weren't sure who the model was? Well, now we know it was Annabelle."

When Gemma groaned, I imagined her rolling her eyes. "And that's significant because?"

When Wendy finished laying it out for her, Gemma was still skeptical but amazingly polite. "I can see Edith leaping to the conclusion that her childhood friend was planning to seduce her daughter and even being angry about it. But angry enough to stab him? That seems a stretch."

"That's pretty much how Ellie felt when we told her. And she suggested we speak with Lavinia to gather more background on Edward's relationships—not just with Edith but with St. John. Leta felt confident St. John was out of the picture, but Ellie was right—more background couldn't hurt."

It was Belle's turn in the spotlight. "With Ellie out of the picture, Leta asked me to join her—probably because I really *am* a little old lady. Lavinia and I got on quite well, and letting her reminisce about Edward paid off."

After elaborating on Lavinia's memories, she concluded with her big aha. "Edith was in love with Edward. That explains everything."

A choking sound came over the phone. "She what?" Gemma had been very patient, but this was a bridge too far. "No offense, Belle, but what on earth makes you think that?"

"No offense taken. Wendy and Leta wondered the same thing until we rehashed everything we'd heard since our arrival."

"Which is why," Wendy said, "we knew we had to talk to Rob. If he told us Edith showed up at home right after her row with Annabelle, the truth of her relationship with Edward wouldn't matter. We'd be back to square one."

I took over. "But he didn't. He was in bed by ten and Edith wasn't there, meaning she had no alibi for the time of Edward's death. Of course, Rob didn't either—but again, no motive. It's funny how the more you learn, the more previous conversations take on heightened importance. I overheard a conversation between Rob and Edith earlier this week. He said Annabelle was a grown woman and to let her be."

Recapping our discussion with Rob didn't take long. "Still, it was hard to fathom Edith stabbing a sleeping man in the back. Why didn't she just read him the riot act? And that's when Wendy decided another visit to Edward's studio was in order."

"And the kitchen door data from Bash clinched the deal," said Wendy.

We had to back up to explain Wendy's lightbulb moment in the studio and the discovery of the keypad by the door. It didn't surprise me that Gemma was momentarily struck dumb when we finished.

"I'm . . . I'm gobsmacked. But it makes sense. And I'll go you one better. What if Edith wasn't just in love with him? What if they slept together?"

Belle clapped her hands. "Exactly what we thought. Do you remember dinner on the first night? Edward described Annabelle as the spitting image of her mother. If she slept with him all those years ago, imagine how that comment made her feel. That would certainly up the ante for her."

"Now that we've identified the killer," I said, "what do we do next, Gemma? Do we just sit tight? Should we three join Sophie and Ellie at the hunting lodge?"

"Let me think, Leta." Silence echoed down the line. "I don't think you're in danger. Even if Edith begins to worry that you're asking lots of questions, it's not as though she can kill you all off."

That's not exactly comforting. "Gee, thanks, Gemma. If she only attacks one or two of us, that will be fine."

In her imitable fashion, Wendy piped up. "What if we lay a trap for her?"

That got a Gemma response I was used to. "Have you lost your mind? Leta's concerned about your safety, and you want to provoke the killer?!"

"As the adult in the room," said Belle, "I suggest we go on as though nothing has changed. We can take it a step further if asked and suggest that the murderer must be an outsider, possibly someone from Edward's life abroad. And that's it. We lay low until you or the local authorities get here."

"Finally, the voice of reason. Thank you, Belle. I'm counting on you to keep Leta and Wendy in line. Hold on." We heard

Gavin in the background. "Mum's being rebellious, and Dad needs my help. Must run."

Pointing at Wendy, I spluttered. "Keep us in line? I *am* in line. She must be talking about you, Wendy Davies."

Belle leaned on her cane and stood. "Enough. Let's have lunch and practice being nonchalant. After that, I suggest we keep a low profile." She glared at her daughter. "No rocking the boat. Are we clear?"

I was relieved when Wendy nodded. Lunch and my book sounded like the ingredients for a much-needed low-key afternoon.

Act nonchalant. How hard could it be?

CHAPTER TWENTY-TWO

BASH HAD HIS HAND raised to knock on the door when I opened it. "Right on time, ladies. We're ready to serve a hearty lunch."

As he pulled our chairs out, he inquired about Ellie. "What have you done with the fourth member of your merry band? Haven't seen her all morning."

Belle smoothly stepped in. "Ellie declared it a day for reading in bed, and she's got her nose buried in a Margery Allingham mystery. I may follow her lead when I go upstairs for my afternoon lie-down."

"Well, the library's packed full of her books and those of other Golden Age authors, so she's in the right place. Now, let me fetch Edith so she can tell you what she's cooked up."

Moments later, Edith bustled in. "It's a soup day, don't you think? We've got leek and potato soup with cheese scones and sausage rolls. And for dessert, there's warm apple crumble with vanilla ice cream. Too bad your vegetarian friend isn't here. I think she would have loved the soup."

When we assured her we were more than ready to dig in, she and Bash disappeared back into the kitchen. When they were out of earshot, Belle leaned in. "We'd better let Ellie know about her sudden devotion to Margery Allingham."

"Good catch, Mum. As far as anyone's concerned, Sophie's in her studio. Beyond us, only Rob knows she and Ellie are together."

Wendy grinned when my phone played its Billy Joel ringtone. "I still want Dave to load a special song on my phone, but I can't settle on the right one."

His cheerful greeting was the perfect way to take the edge off the tense morning. "Hi, sweetheart. How goes it?"

In the hall, I gave him the lowdown as succinctly as I could. "The upshot is that Belle's in charge until the authorities get here. I'm sure you can figure out who the problem child will be."

"I know it won't be you or Ellie—as long as you keep Ellie away from her shotgun, that is. Do you think Wendy will toe the line?"

We debated the likelihood of her listening to Belle and decided she was more likely to listen to her than to me or Gemma. "Anyway, I'm looking forward to reading and napping and enjoying a roaring fire with Dickens. Got to run so I don't miss lunch. Love you."

The soup and scones hit the spot, and I split a sausage roll with Wendy to save room for dessert. "If I have another bite, I'll fall into a food coma."

Wendy touched her napkin to her lips. "I'm with you, but I'm not missing out on apple crumble. And I want the soup recipe from Edith before diving back into Dorothy Sayers. You're

reading Ngaio Marsh, right?" Beatrix, our local bookshop owner, had assigned Golden Age authors for our January book club
meeting instead of a single book, and we were savoring the variety.

By the time I finished my half of dessert, I knew I had to have
the recipe, too. "Dave would adore this apple crumble. You know
what a fiend he is for sweets." Belle headed upstairs with a parting
admonishment not to disturb her until dinner.

In the kitchen, Edith was chopping vegetables. Her calm demeanor almost made me think twice about our suspicions, but
the conversation took a turn when the mudroom door creaked
open, and Annabelle came up the stairs to the kitchen, her cheeks
flushed from the cold.

"Mum, do you have it ready? Dad's starving."

Edith pointed to the sideboard. "There's the tray. And what
are you doing in my kitchen in those muddy boots?"

Rolling her eyes, Annabelle scratched Dickens behind the
ears. "Hello, ladies. Did you enjoy your lunch?"

Wendy held up a recipe card. "So much so, that we want all the
recipes."

Edith clapped a hand to her forehead. "I completely forgot to
send something up to Ellie. She'll be starving."

Wendy and I glanced at each other, but before we could react,
Annabelle spoke up. "Didn't they tell you, Mum? Ellie's at the
hunting lodge. Dad took her up earlier, but she's all set. He took
her food too."

Words tumbled from my mouth, and I prayed they made
sense. "She's been reminiscing about visiting here with Nigel,
and the hunting lodge played a big part in her memories. Sounds

as though she decided to sneak off and have a quiet day there instead of in her room."

Edith's eyes narrowed. "And she didn't tell any of you? How odd."

Wendy came up with a rejoinder. "Probably didn't want us intruding on her solitude. I'm glad Rob was around to help her out."

With a shrug, Annabelle grabbed the tray. "Dad didn't say it was a secret. Sorry if I spoiled anything."

She started toward the steps before turning back. "Were Dad and I the last of your interviews? If so, I'm going for a short ride before more snow comes in. Want to join me?"

Before I could refuse, Edith blurted, "Interviews? What interviews?"

That wasn't a question I wanted to answer. "Just simple ones. Gemma asked us to jot down anything fresh in people's minds until the police could get here."

Wendy added. "We're convinced it's someone from Edward's past, maybe from his life in France. Gemma will pick up from there."

As Edith's gaze darted between us, her expression unreadable, my pulse quickened. Did she suspect we were hiding something?

Annabelle's laughter broke the tension. "Mum, has no one told you about the Little Old Ladies' Detective Agency? I admit I thought it was a joke when Sophie told me about it."

To my horror, Annabelle explained that she'd Googled us and discovered several articles in *The Astonbury Aha*. I tried not to react as I heard the words housekeeper, magician, and dog nappers. So much for keeping a low profile. When Wendy took that as her cue to provide color commentary, I nearly leapt from my chair. If

I could have stuffed the words back in her mouth, I would have. *What was she thinking?*

As Edith's expression shifted between curiosity and unease, I made an elaborate show of yawning. "I can barely keep my eyes open, and I blame you, Edith. Lunch was heavenly, and I stuffed myself. It's definitely time for a nap."

"Who are you kidding, Leta? You're famous for your naps, but today, I think I'll take one, too." Wendy followed me through the dining room door, chuckling.

I managed to hold my tongue until we reached the drawing room. "What on earth were you thinking?"

"Calm down, Leta. I have a plan."

CHAPTER TWENTY-THREE

THE ONLY ONE WHO managed a nap that afternoon was Belle. Wendy was off to investigate Rob's slip about the hunting lodge, and Ellie had taken Sophie under her wing to prep her for the evening. My task? Transforming the drawing room per Wendy's instructions.

She returned looking relieved. "Annabelle caught Rob off guard when she asked about the ATV tracks. He didn't mention Sophie, though—only Ellie. Smart man."

We worked in companionable silence, clearing the taped pages from the wall, filling a file folder, and tidying up. At last, Wendy stood back, satisfied. "Belle's next. She needs to know her lines."

Throwing on my coat, I woke Dickens for a walk. I let him run ahead as I carefully descended the stone steps. The second band of snow was heavier than the first, and the steps were treacherous. Not to Dickens, of course. Thankful that I still had time for a long soak in my tub, I indulged in throwing snowballs for him until I could no longer feel my toes.

Bash grinned as he offered me a towel from the front desk. "Leta, guess who's coming to dinner?" The movie with Sidney Poitier and Spencer Tracy immediately came to mind, but I doubted Bash had ever heard of it. "Sophie and I are going to help Edith with dinner, and we're trying to talk Emilia into building a snowman with us afterward."

That told me that Ellie had completed her first task. Per Wendy's plan, Sophie and Bash would be together all evening and hopefully overnight. After dinner and a snowman, Sophie would lock herself in her flat, hopefully with Bash.

"Good plan, Bash. With the forecast calling for warm temps and sunshine tomorrow, this may be your last chance. We're going to head home once the roads are passable, so this will be our final night."

As instructed, I dressed in the outfit I'd packed for our farewell dinner, and Dickens wore his bow tie. We were booked for another two nights, but we had agreed we were ready to get home. At least, that was the story we planned to give out. To be convincing, we needed to dress the part. The weather forecast played into our hands, predicting the temps would rise enough the next day to make our departure feasible.

Belle and Ellie were all smiles as I joined them in the dining room. In her pale blue floor-length skirt with the matching satin jacket, Belle reminded me of Geraldine McEwan, my favorite Miss Marple actress.

Rob had fetched Sophie and Ellie in plenty of time for our dowager countess to outfit herself in fancy dress. She wore a rhinestone-trimmed black velvet pantsuit and had pinned one side of her silver pageboy back with a matching comb. When Wendy arrived in her aqua beaded dress, Act One was ready to begin.

As if on cue, Bash entered from the kitchen to seat us and light the candles in the delicate candelabra at our table. Tonight, he wore a tux and had a white napkin draped over his arm.

He surprised us when he pointed to the wine cooler stand next to our table. "Compliments of the house, ladies. We couldn't let you leave without a proper sendoff." As he uncorked the bottle of champagne, Sophie appeared with a tray of oysters Rockefeller.

We carried on a lively conversation as we demolished the oysters and the French onion soup that followed. Nothing of consequence was discussed. The topics ran the gamut—the snow, the horses, how we loved our rooms, and the barn. Wendy hadn't scripted us, but she'd advised us to keep it light and cheerful.

After the roast chicken was served, we lowered our voices and kept a close eye on the kitchen door. To all appearances, we were discussing something confidential. When Edith came through the door, Wendy made a show of shushing us. "Hello, Edith, you've outdone yourself again."

"Thank you. It's my pleasure. I'm sorry to hear you're cutting your visit short, but I understand. I *do* hope you'll return."

Ellie smiled at me. "I expect you'll see plenty of Leta, as she's booked a December wedding, and, of course, we'll all be here for that."

That was true. I had plenty to discuss with Bash. "And I plan to pick your brain for menu suggestions, Edith. I know I'll be in good hands."

"Speaking of menus, I hear Ellie and I missed out on an opportunity to go through your recipes," said Belle. "May we visit with you after dinner?"

"Of course. And you can let me know whether you'd like something special for breakfast tomorrow, it being your last one. The larder's still full, so I can whip up pretty much anything."

As she turned to leave, she reminded us to save room for dessert. It was then that Wendy leaned in, her voice just loud enough. "Leta, Edith's a jewel. I know you're obsessed with the argument she and Annabelle had, but I think you need to let it go."

Ellie waited until Edith was through the door. "She heard you, Wendy. She did a stutter-step at the door and glanced back. Now, it's up to Belle and me."

I was almost too nervous to enjoy my trifle, but not quite. When we'd cleaned our plates, we split up—Belle and Ellie to the kitchen, and Wendy and me to the drawing room.

Once we had the fire going, Dickens flopped by the hearth, and I couldn't help smiling when he immediately began snoring. Wendy and I were too keyed up to relax, much less doze off. I poured two glasses of Kahlua. "If Belle and Ellie pull off their part, we'll have company before the night's over."

"Oh, I have every confidence they will. I provided plenty of ideas, and you know they'll ad lib as needed. I expect they'll be here soon to let us know what they wound up saying."

Sipping her Kahlua, Wendy studied the large piece of paper taped above the mantel. I'd had to stand on a chair to get it up there. In big, bold letters, I'd captured our conclusions.

EDITH: Confronts Edward—fumes—finds painting in studio—stabs Edward

MOTIVE: Loved him—slept with him(?)—posed for him—fears he'll seduce Annabelle

"This is perfect, Leta."

Before I could respond, a soft knock interrupted us, and Wendy let Belle and Ellie in. "Perfect timing. We're dying to know how it went. Did she fall for it?"

Ellie dropped into the overstuffed chair while Belle perched on the loveseat, propping her cane on the arm. Dickens promptly claimed her feet as his new pillow. "It went like clockwork," Ellie said. "Though I must say, Leta, you owe us for this one. Edith wasn't exactly eager to chat."

"Me? This is all Wendy's doing."

Belle's eyes gleamed. "Trust me, luv, I know that, but I think it was a grand plan. We gave Edith plenty to think about. Of course, we told her that Ellie and I were experts at reuniting lost dogs with their owners, and that you two fancied yourselves as Agatha Raisin and Tuppence."

"Right," said Ellie. "She took that in stride. It was when we launched into how you identify and eliminate suspects that things got interesting. We painted Leta as the ringleader—completely obsessive about finding answers."

"Obsessive?" I said, feigning offense.

"You know it's true," Wendy teased. "Keep going, Mum."

"We told her Leta had been harping on the mother-daughter argument."

Belle winked at me. "You know, Leta, how you claimed your mother would *never* have dared to interfere in your life like that. Edith didn't bite at first, but when Ellie described you filling the drawing room with notes and theories, she started paying attention."

The corners of Ellie's mouth turned up. "I might have mentioned the mess you make when you're in full-on detective mode, and Belle added a bit about your process—flipcharts, notebooks, the whole nine yards. And how you spend hours on possibilities before striking a suspect from the list—unless, of course, you unearth some new clue."

I squirmed. "This is hard to listen to. I sure hope it worked."

"Oh, it did." Ellie said. "She kept asking if you were serious, and we just shrugged it off. Said you and Wendy were hashing things out in here as we spoke, and we were happy to stay out of it."

"And" Belle added with a sly grin, "we never let up on your fixation on the argument. You have a feeling the mother-daughter disagreement is significant, but you can't put your finger on what it is about it that bothers you. It's clear to me and Ellie that, as someone who's never had children, you just don't get it. If she wasn't worried before, she is now."

I rubbed my temple. It was funny, but it wasn't. "You two are impossible."

Belle lifted her chin. "We're good, if I do say so myself. The upshot is Edith thinks you're in here building a case for her as the murderer, so that you can share your findings with Gemma."

With an exaggerated wink, Ellie summed up. "And I know you won't believe it, but Belle and I were at a loss to provide answers as to what evidence you have. She won't be able to resist sneaking in here to see what you've been working on. And since we did such a good job describing the mess you two make by papering the walls with your outlandish ideas . . . well, let's just say, she took the bait."

Wendy rubbed her hands together. "Step into my parlor, said the spider to the fly."

CHAPTER TWENTY-FOUR

W<small>RAPPED IN THE DOWN</small> comforter from my bed, I huddled on the floor behind the front desk with Dickens. "Remember, not a sound." I looked at my watch. It was 11:30 and still no sign of Edith. Had Wendy's elaborate trap failed?

When the lights went out a few minutes later, it seemed an eternity before they flickered back on. I was in mid-yawn when I heard someone approaching from the dining room. If it turned out to be Bash, I'd be sorely disappointed. As whoever it was padded quietly across the great hall, the lights flickered, and then . . . they went out.

In the sudden silence, I heard the wind howling outside but nothing else. I risked peeking over the top of the desk and, to my surprise, saw that the snow reflecting the light of the moon made it easy to see Edith standing stock-still in front of the drawing room door.

If I were a character in a mystery novel, the words, "Leta waited with bated breath," would appear. When Edith turned the knob and pushed the door open, she stood framed in the glow of the fireplace. Did she wonder why the fire was still going strong? Or was she focused on the large piece of paper above it? Could she read the words in the dim light coming through the window? Her gasp gave me the answer.

I'd second-guessed her motive even as I'd written it out. The timing for the evening left little doubt in my mind that she was the killer. But do you stab a man in cold blood because you slept with him and think your daughter will too? But now, I knew we were right. Edith was standing in the drawing room for a reason.

When the lights popped back on, my instincts kicked in. I crossed to the drawing room in my stocking feet, Dickens by my side. It was then that Edith turned toward the window, where a Tiffany lamp glowed on a small round table. I was sure she'd spotted the manila file folder Wendy had prepared—a folder with the name Gemma scrawled across it.

Two things happened simultaneously. Edith reached the table, and Wendy came out from behind the curtains. Edith froze, as though she couldn't decide whether to make a quick exit or stay and bluff her way through.

"Now, Dickens."

One moment, he was standing by my side, and the next he growled low in his throat and bounded into the room, planting himself firmly between me and Edith. His hackles rose as he bared his teeth. My first thought was that he deserved an Oscar for his performance.

Wendy confronted her. "Edith, what are you doing in here?"

Edith's face was pale, but her tone was defiant. "I need to know what lies you've been cooking up about me."

"Lies?" Wendy snapped as she stepped from behind the curtain. "We're trying to figure out who killed Edward, and you being here doesn't exactly look innocent."

Stumbling backward, Edith looked toward the door. "You . . . you don't understand."

I placed a hand on Dickens's head to calm him. "Then explain it to us."

Her reaction was a mix of defeat and belligerence—her shoulders slumped, and then her voice rose. "You're sure you've got it all figured out, aren't you? But you don't know the half of it."

"Then tell us," Wendy bluffed. "Because whatever secret you're keeping, it's not going to stay hidden much longer. We already know you were there that night, in the spa."

Edith sobbed. "It's not just my secret. It's Edward's, though he never knew. And Annabelle's. And Rob's."

Is this it? Is she going to reveal the real motive? "What do you mean?"

"Annabelle isn't Rob's daughter," she whispered. "She's Edward's."

The words hung in the air, heavy and shocking. Wendy and I were speechless.

"I was young and stupid. We were best friends . . . until that summer. Edward was charming, and I thought it meant something. But it was just a fling to him. Another conquest." She shook her head. "After his accident, everything changed. And when I found out I was pregnant, I married Rob. I knew the timing was off, but he never questioned it—never doubted she was his."

I remembered what Lavinia had said. The riding accident was a life-changing event for him, and he never looked back. "Edward never knew?"

"No," Edith gasped. "And neither does Annabelle. I wanted to keep it that way. But then Edward came back, and I saw the way he looked at her. The way he flirted. He didn't know, but I did. And I couldn't let him sleep with his . . . our daughter."

Wendy found her voice. "Couldn't you have told him the truth, that Annabelle was his daughter?"

"No! He would never have kept it to himself. And the truth would have killed Rob and Annabelle."

She sank onto the loveseat, and Dickens, sensing the change in her, leaned against her leg. "I just wanted to talk to him, to make him stop. I begged him to leave her alone, but he just laughed and accused me of being jealous. She was an adult, he said, and could make her own choices. It wasn't my place to interfere."

Did we get it wrong? Did she kill him then and there? "And the dagger?" I asked. "Did you see it and grab it?"

"No, not then. I left. It wasn't until I went to the studio." She pointed to the page over the mantle. "I saw the painting. My daughter, the way he'd captured her—she never stood a chance."

The taunts, the painting—it had all been too much. She closed her eyes as if replaying the scene. "I told myself I was only going back to reason with him. But when I saw him lying there, smug and untouchable, something inside me broke."

She brought her hands to her lips. "The dagger was there, on display. It wasn't even a conscious thought. I only knew I couldn't let him destroy my family. And it was over before I knew it."

Speaking gently, Wendy placed a hand on Edith's shoulder. "It's over now. But you need to tell the truth. For Annabelle's sake."

Edith looked up. "The truth will break her heart—and Rob's too. But you're right. It's time."

CHAPTER TWENTY-FIVE

THE LITTLE OLD LADIES' Detective Agency had been instrumental in solving several crimes—twelve, to be exact. And each time, the authorities swooped in to take over, and, I might add, to take the credit. Not this time.

Leaving Wendy to keep an eye on Edith, I sat on the steps and attempted to think clearly. Without Gemma on-site or on the way, we were faced with several critical questions—what to do with Edith, for starters. Next, we had to figure out when to tell the family. Should we wait for Gemma to notify them that it was Edith, their beloved cook, who had murdered Edward? Or tell them ourselves? If the job fell to us, how *much* should we tell them?

Was it our place to tell Lavinia she'd lost a son but gained a granddaughter? Shouldn't Edith's family learn that Edward was Annabelle's father before anyone else did? What if Edith changed her mind about telling them?

And then there was the whole tale of Edward as a jewel thief. Because it was Sophie who identified him as one of her father's accomplices, telling the family would mean betraying her secret. That situation had nothing to do with Edward's death. Did the family even need to know?

In the end, we worked it out, but it took some doing. Calling Gemma to tell her we'd secured a confession was one thing. Explaining how was another thing entirely.

As I held the phone away from my ear, I reminded myself that enduring her expletive-filled reaction to what prompted the confession was a small price to pay. After all, we'd solved the case. I only wished I could have recorded Gemma's reaction for Wendy to hear.

When Gemma calmed down enough to think straight, we came up with a plan. First, I woke Ellie. She called her son Matthew in Astonbury and put him in charge of transporting Gemma to Deddington as soon as the snow stopped falling. In his ancient Land Rover, the trip to Deddington would be doable, just barely.

We concluded that Edith wasn't a danger to anyone, except possibly herself. Her love for Annabelle was probably enough to keep her from contemplating suicide, but we didn't want to take any chances. When Ellie suggested my room as the best place to hold her, I balked. "No way. If I can see my way clear to getting married here after all this, the last thing I want is to spend my wedding night picturing a murderer in my room."

Wendy's room was the eventual choice, with Wendy and Belle on guard duty. Keeping Edith hidden kept us from having to deliver the news to the family. That could wait until Gemma arrived.

Next came dealing with Rob. I set my alarm so I could call him at 5:30 to say Edith had stayed overnight at the manor house, and she hadn't wanted to call and wake him. He was curious but too busy with the horses to push me. By 6:15, I'd let Dickens out for a romp in the snow and was in the kitchen with Ellie, drinking coffee and working on a breakfast menu.

When her phone chirped with a text from Matthew, we breathed a sigh of relief. The sun hadn't yet risen, but he and Gemma were on their way.

They arrived shortly after seven, and we were surprised when a Jeep pulled in behind them. Gemma had called in support from the Chipping Norton Police Station, and they 'd sent a constable and a family liaison officer. How like Gemma to think of that.

After Edith was escorted to the drawing room, it wasn't long before Gemma requested my presence. "Leta, she's very subdued, but she's told me essentially the same thing she told you. Her only request is that I allow her to tell her family the truth about Edward before they hear it from someone else. Given the circumstances, I'm going to let her do that before I meet with the Foxbournes."

I couldn't stop my mind from racing as I watched Gemma and the FLO traverse the snow-covered grounds with Edith. How would Rob and Annabelle react? Could they forgive her? What would this revelation do to the family? Especially Annabelle, who would learn that the man her mother had killed—the man she considered a kindly uncle—was, in fact, her father.

Deep in thought, I was startled when Ellie put her hand on my shoulder. Belle and Wendy were standing behind her. "Come along, Leta. All we can do now is wait."

We were a somber group as we kept watch from the dining room windows, and it was a welcome relief when Dickens barked, "It's Lucky." Sure enough, the grey dog was streaking our way.

When Dickens ran to the front door, I followed and grabbed my coat. The two dogs greeted each other, but they didn't break into their usual playful antics. Instead, they walked slowly side by side, as though they'd picked up on the mood. Of course they had. Dickens knew what had transpired the night before, and Lucky had surely been privy to the conversation at the stables.

In the distance, a group of five trudged through the snow. Seeing Rob with his arm around Edith made me think all the more of him. Stalwart was the word that came to mind. No matter the circumstances, he wasn't forsaking Edith. How Annabelle was handling the shock, I couldn't tell.

Leaving the FLO with the family, Gemma hastened toward me. "Leta, Edith wants to speak with you."

Why, I wondered, as I squared my shoulders. When the group reached the Jeep, Edith spoke in Rob's ear and came forward without him. Her face was pale but composed. "Leta, please tell Wendy she was right. Annabelle deserved to know the truth, no matter how much it hurt. I just pray she can forgive me someday."

"She will. You did what you thought was best, Edith. Now it's time to let the truth do its work." Taking her hand, I walked with her to the car where Rob stood with his arm around Annabelle.

Her voice trembling but firm, Edith spoke to her family. "I'm so sorry for everything. I love you more than you'll ever know." With that she turned, and the constable helped her into the car.

Bash stood with his nose pressed to the long narrow window flanking the front door. When he didn't immediately accost us, I knew the shock of seeing Edith taken away had rendered him speechless. His mouth gaping, he looked from me to Gemma.

We'd kept him at bay earlier by putting him to work delivering breakfast to his family. In response to his question about where Edith was, we simply said we'd let her sleep in. That was true. Somehow, she had finally dropped into a fitful sleep in Wendy's room.

Gemma took charge. "Bash, I'll explain what's going on to you and the rest of the family shortly. Can you sit tight a bit longer? And please don't share what you just witnessed."

When he nodded mutely, she motioned me to the dining room. "I saw the other three by the window in there, and I need to know exactly what's been said to whom this morning. Not to mention, I could do with more coffee."

She led off by asking what had been said to Edith overnight. That answer was simple enough. Wendy and Belle hadn't disclosed a thing. They'd seen it as their responsibility to keep Edith calm, nothing more. From there, we moved to the questions that had troubled me since the confrontation in the drawing room.

We dealt with the easy decisions first. Edward's jewel thefts should be revealed only if necessary. Other than Sophie, Charlotte was the only person who knew about the earrings, and she'd already half convinced herself Edward had good intentions. Sophie's story wasn't relevant to the murder. The accusations about Edward stealing jewelry from his paramours were also irrelevant.

All that remained was the why, and Belle had a strong opinion about that. "Annabelle's paternity is not our secret to tell."

We readily agreed that the family deserved to know why Edith had killed her childhood friend and that the short answer would have to do. She did it to protect Annabelle. Gemma would have to explain what that meant without revealing Annabelle's paternity—unless the family explicitly asked.

Belle brought up Lavinia. "Gemma, be prepared that Lavinia may put two and two together when she reflects on that last summer before everything changed, as she puts it. She may not ask today, but I suspect she will later."

Gemma closed her eyes. "Edward's artwork and his reputation for seducing the women he painted are the building blocks for Edith's motive. It's believable that she feared her daughter would fall prey to his charms and have her heart broken. It's not as powerful a motive as the full story, but it's enough to give the family closure."

As we waited for the Foxbournes to gather in the drawing room, Gemma pulled Wendy and me aside. "Let me be clear—I strongly disapprove of the trap you laid. Do you understand the danger you put yourselves in? Did you even think of all the ways it could have gone wrong?"

That scolding was followed by an exasperated breath. "Despite your rash behavior, you deserve to be present when I speak with the family. You've built a rapport with them, and they're bound to ask you questions after I leave. I trust you enough to know you won't say anything you shouldn't."

She cleared her throat. "One more thing. Without Edith's confession, it's unlikely we would have had the evidence to charge her." A frown appeared on her face. "As much as it pains me to say it—thank you."

I was stunned. There had been occasions when Gemma complimented us on discovering a nugget that she found helpful—and then, in the same breath, called me a nosey parker. But this was quite possibly the first time she'd uttered the words *thank you* without a disclaimer. I could tell by the look on Wendy's face that she was thinking the same thing.

The Foxbourne family took their seats, all of them wearing somber expressions, and Gemma got right to it. "There's no other way to say this. We've arrested the person responsible for Edward's death. That person is Edith Thompson."

After the gasps and expressions of disbelief died down, she outlined Edith's confession. Her worry over what she saw as Edward's predatory behavior toward Annabelle. How she'd tried to discourage her daughter from spending time with him to no avail. How she'd seen his sketches at Annabelle's cottage and assumed the worst.

She ticked off the sequence of events. Edith confronted him, and Edward was dismissive, even suggested she was jealous. She found the painting in the studio—and it reminded her of his Lady Godiva series. And that led to her stabbing him.

"I believe her when she says she intended only to confront him. That doesn't change what she did. It only indicates that her actions were impulsive, rather than premeditated."

There was no doubt that they were shocked. Bash clenched his jaw. Emilia held her hand to her mouth, her eyes wide. Charlotte whispered *no*.

It was St. John who spoke first. "They grew up together. She's been part of this estate, this family, her whole life. It's . . . how do I describe it? I can't believe it."

A sob escaped Lavinia. "Edward always had a way of causing trouble, even when he didn't mean to. But Edith . . . I never thought . . ."

Emilia asked about the painting, and Gemma deferred to me and Wendy because she hadn't seen it. I was glad we were there to provide more detail and describe it as tasteful yet suggestive. "I can see that," she said.

Bash seemed to be struggling the most. As though every word was a hammer blow chipping away at his image of his uncle. And of Edith.

When there was nothing more to say, St. John thanked Gemma and helped his mother to her feet. He turned back at the doorway. "Leta, I'd be grateful if you could find time to speak with me before you leave this afternoon."

The door to St. John's study was cracked open, and when I poked my head in, he motioned to the chair in front of his desk. He looked haggard.

"I want to thank you for whatever part you played in unmasking Edward's murderer." He rubbed his forehead. "I still find it hard to say that word, much less to think it was Edith."

What could I say but "you're welcome?" I knew there was more to why he wanted to see me, so I sat quietly until he got to it.

"I am not unaware of the conversations you've had with my family and the staff, and I suspect you've uncovered some unsavory truths about my brother. Am I correct?"

At my nod, he continued. "Did your discoveries include the accusations made against him?"

"If you mean that he stole jewelry from several women, yes, but they didn't have any bearing on his death, so we didn't pursue it at length."

I took advantage of his silence to satisfy my curiosity. "St. John, did his wife's heirs in France level any accusations against Edward? Perchance to do with her jewelry?"

He gave me a quizzical look. "You know about that? The daughters accused him of taking a sapphire choker and matching earrings. That was another situation that required a solicitor."

So, Edward had been truthful with Sophie about the origins of the choker. Whether the daughters ever received matching necklaces was something we'd likely never know.

St. John drummed his fingers on the desk. "Let me be direct. Is there a need to mention any of this to my mother?"

I clasped my hands on the desk. "No, St. John. I've learned that all manner of things come to light in investigations like this, and I liken the process to pulling on loose threads in search of the one that will unravel the crime. We consider and set aside lots of information, and that's the case here. Sharing those accusations with your mother would only cause her pain."

"Thank you for that, Leta. I've shielded her from so much for just that reason. Edward never hid his peccadilloes, and she's always taken them in stride, even made light of them. I'd like for her memories of him as a lovable scamp to remain intact."

He was satisfied, but I wasn't. I couldn't shake the feeling that Lavinia deserved to know she had another granddaughter.

Midsummer at Foxbourne Park

I'd gone back and forth as to whether I would feel comfortable holding the wedding at Foxbourne Park. When Dave and I listed the pros and cons, it quickly boiled down to one point on each side. The murder was the obvious con, and Dave pointed out that the single most important pro was I'd fallen in love with the barn as the perfect spot. True to form, he said it was no problem to carry on the search if that was what I wanted.

In the end, it was talking with Ellie that pushed me to stick with the plan. Her description of the look on my face when I first saw the interior of the barn convinced me I'd never find anything more perfect. "Leta, it's what you read about in novels. Your face really did light up. You twirled in place taking in the twinkling lights, smiling all the while. It's not an exaggeration to say your eyes sparkled."

This was my second trip back to meet with Bash about the wedding. With the help of a wedding planner, we'd settled on the flowers, the musicians, everything but the menu for the reception. Now that Caroline, Ellie's cook, had accepted the job as the chef at Foxbourne Park, I was here to finalize that.

Bash greeted me as I opened the front door. "Leta, I was hoping to intercept you before you went to the kitchen. I'm sure Caroline won't mind if you're a few minutes late."

Beaming, he escorted me to his office behind the front desk. "I wanted you to hear it from me first. Sophie and I are engaged."

"Why, Bash, that's wonderful news. I'm delighted for you both."

"Thank you. Sophie said to be sure to tell you that she could never have accepted my proposal if not for you."

"Me? What did I have to do with it?"

He explained that they'd both taken Edward's death hard but for different reasons. It wasn't until after the funeral that Sophie shared her story with him. "She told me that speaking with you helped her to see that she had to tell me about her father . . . and Uncle Edward . . . that our relationship couldn't last with that secret hanging between us."

What a brave young woman. I hadn't counseled her to reveal the truth to Bash, but she had figured out on her own that she had to.

"Leta, on the heels of his death, it was a dreadful blow to learn those things about Uncle Edward. And it broke my heart to hear how he'd treated Sophie. Worst of all, though, was when she looked at me and said she would understand if I wanted her to leave. Can you imagine? Nothing her father or Uncle Edward did changes how I feel about Sophie, and that's what I told her. Even then, she was worried about how Mum and Dad would react."

"And? Did you share the story with them?"

"Only when Sophie pushed me. She'd already told Emilia and Annabelle. Emilia's reaction was just like mine. She was more disappointed in Uncle Edward than anything else. So, I took it to Dad, and I guess you know how he reacted."

As I thought about what St. John knew about his brother, I doubted the new revelations had come as a surprise. Still, hearing the sordid details must have shaken him.

Bash confirmed my assumption. "The first words out of his mouth were 'I should have known.' When he told me what he already knew, it was like putting puzzle pieces in place."

Together, father and son had decided it was best not to share Sophie's revelations with Charlotte and Lavinia. With three members of the family now in the know, I suspected it would eventually come out, but it was not my worry to deal with.

Bash leaned closer. "Leta, you won't believe what came next. Dad smiled and said, 'You love her, don't you?' I thought I'd kept my feelings under wraps, but obviously not."

When Bash confessed he not only loved Sophie but intended to marry her, St. John shared the where and how of his proposal to Charlotte, and from there, a plan was hatched to pop the question at the same spot—the gazebo.

"I didn't want the cloud of Uncle Edward's death to taint what I hoped would be the joy of my proposal, so I waited a few months. I took Sophie to dinner and then suggested a ride in the golfcart to the gazebo. Thanks to Emilia and Annabelle, it was strung with lanterns and flowers. Sophie was speechless, and when I led her up the steps and got down on one knee . . . she said yes!"

I was still grinning when I arrived in the kitchen. It was clear that Caroline had given lots of thought to my holiday wedding menu, and only one or two adjustments were needed. Her creative menu even gave a nod to my Greek heritage with bite-size spanakopita and tiropita triangles.

I was surprised when Lavinia joined us as we were wrapping up and delighted when she invited me for lemonade in the garden. This was high season, but she showed me to a secluded spot shaded by a pergola covered in climbing roses.

After we'd been served lemonade and petits fours, we chatted about how quickly Caroline had settled in and, in particular, her flair for coming up with creative wedding menus. Word of mouth about her special touches had resulted in several new bookings.

"Leta, have you heard that we'll be celebrating a family wedding here next summer? Bash finally popped the question to Sophie."

"He just told me, and I'm so happy for them. I could tell he was head over heels when we were here."

"Yes, and I'm proud of Charlotte for admitting her objections were ridiculous. I think the turning point may have been when Sophie offered to reset her emerald earrings in a simpler design as Edward had suggested. Charlotte says she smiles every time she wears them."

She refilled our glasses. "You know, Leta, it's strange how life works. After all these months, I find myself looking at Annabelle not just as Edith's daughter, but as my granddaughter."

My jaw dropped before my face broke into a smile. "I can't tell you how happy I am that you know. We wrestled over whether to tell you, but thought it wasn't our place."

Her eyes twinkled. "Do you know how I found out?"

"I'm wondering if Edith told you."

"No, it was Bash, of all people. One evening, he came into the library looking unusually serious. When I asked him what was troubling him, he hesitated, before saying, 'Gran, there's something you should know about Annabelle.' Of course, with all that's gone on, I was afraid it would be something dreadful."

As I pictured Bash sitting beside her, I couldn't think of a better person to share the news that she had a third grandchild.

"You probably know that he, Sophie, and Annabelle are fast friends. He told me Sophie had encouraged Annabelle to confide in him. And then Bash, bless him, thought I had a right to know as well. Annabelle was hesitant. She was worried about how I would take it and was even considering moving away. Bash convinced her I'd be devastated if I found out some other way. But you know, Leta, in a way I already knew."

I'd never forgotten how she described that fateful summer to Belle. She *did* know. "Bash has a good head on his shoulders. I'm so glad he came to you."

A sad smile crossed Lavinia's face. "For a moment I was shocked, and I could barely breathe. But then the pieces fell into place. I looked at Annabelle the next day, really looked at her, and I saw Edward. Yes, she's the spitting image of Edith with her strawberry blonde hair, but she also has Edward's spark, his joie de vivre. And I realized something—gaining a granddaughter is a gift, even if it comes with sorrow."

"That's a generous way to look at it, Lavinia. Not everyone would find that kind of grace."

"Well, if these last few months have taught me anything, it's that we can't change the past. But we can decide how to move forward. Annabelle is part of this family, and I'll do my best to make sure she feels it."

"I think Edward would be glad she has a place here."

"And she always will. The two of us are still feeling our way, but we'll get there."

On my first return visit, I'd learned that St. John had hired a solicitor for Edith and that she was awaiting trial under strict bail conditions. She and Rob were living in a cottage on the other side of the village.

Lavinia's gaze drifted toward the roses overhead. "Life doesn't stand still to let us make sense of everything. But Annabelle and I and the rest of the family? We'll pick up the pieces, together."

Taking in the serene smile on Lavinia's face, I let the moment settle. For the first time since everything had unfolded, I felt a sense of peace at Foxbourne Park.

CHAPTER TWENTY-SIX

DECEMBER

The barn had never looked more beautiful. Strings of twinkling lights crisscrossed the high wooden beams overhead, casting a golden glow that felt warm and welcoming. The archway at the end of the aisle was draped in white flowers and ivy, with burgundy roses nestled here and there—elegant, understated, perfect. At the wedding planner's suggestion, Bash had added forest green draperies around the sides of the large space, transforming the central area into an intimate chapel.

I took one final look at my reflection and couldn't help but smile. My dress felt like something from a fairy tale—a rich burgundy velvet gown that flowed gracefully to the floor in an elegant A-line silhouette. The long sleeves, accented with removable white fur cuffs, were perfectly suited for a December wedding, and the low sweetheart neckline framed my simple garnet pendant beautifully. The crowning touch was a small fascinator adorned with velvet poinsettia blossoms.

Holding my bouquet of white roses and burgundy hellebores, I peeked through the curtains at the back. Wendy stood by my side, her emerald green gown shimmering in the glow from the lights.

I breathed deeply as the pianist began to play the tender melody Dave had chosen. Hearing the lyrics to "Til There Was You" brought a lump in my throat, and I hummed softly to the words that spoke of love that would last as long as the stars hung in the sky.

As the song came to an end, Wendy adjusted the green ribbon around her bouquet and gave me a quick, reassuring smile. "Ready?" she asked softly.

"I should be asking you that. You're going first."

Her lips twitched into a grin. "Don't worry, I'll make sure I don't trip. I'll leave that to Dickens."

The comment was enough to calm my nerves, and we both laughed quietly. When the pianist struck the opening chords of Pachelbel's "Canon in D Major", Wendy squeezed my hand and stepped through the curtains. The final notes faded away as she reached the archway and took her place opposite Dave and Dickens.

It was my turn.

I stepped forward to the sound of "Here Comes the Bride", alone but not lonely. With every step, I saw someone who was important in my life, someone who had been part of my journey.

Peter and Lucy sat close together, Lucy's hand tucked securely in his. In the same row, Jake had his arm around Gemma and winked at me as I passed. Belle and Ellie sat together in front of them—Belle wore a big smile, and Ellie's eyes sparkled with tears. Beside Ellie were her son Matthew and his wife Sarah.

To my right, I glimpsed Beatrix and Toby with Rhiannon, who was struggling to hold Christie's velvet cushion steady. When the little minx stood on her hind legs, Beatrix tapped her nose and whispered something that made her meow. And there, near the front, were Gavin and Libby. It was at their cocktail party at the inn that I'd first met Dave.

Our families sat in the front rows. Seated together with their husbands were my sisters, Sophia and Anna, here to witness the start of my new life. On the opposite side sat Dave's mom and his sister Michelle, who had welcomed me with open arms. His mother couldn't stop smiling as she glanced from me to Dave.

And then, there he was. When I finally reached him, he extended his hand. "You're beautiful," he whispered as I placed my hand in his.

I heard the officiant's voice, calm and steady. "We are gathered here today to witness and celebrate the union of Leta and Dave in marriage. They stand before us, surrounded by those who have shaped their lives and shared their journey—friends who are like family, family who are like friends.

"Theirs is a love that was patient, persistent, and, like all the best things in life, a little unexpected. Today, they declare that love, commit their lives to each other, and step into the future as partners in every sense of the word."

When Dickens let out a quiet bark, Dave glanced down at him with a grin, then back to me, as though to say, *See? The best man approves.*

And when the officiant finally said, "You may kiss the bride," I smiled as Dave leaned in.

Beneath the twinkling lights, he tilted my chin up and surprised me with a long, lingering kiss. His face broke into a grin as he whispered, "To have, to hold, and to kiss."

When he laced his fingers through mine, we turned to face our friends and family. "The Wedding March" started, and Dickens and Wendy followed behind us. I could've sworn Christie rolled her eyes.

Almost unnoticed as we were being embraced and congratulated, the barn was transformed. Where, moments ago, I'd walked down the aisle under twinkling lights, the space now glowed with soft candlelight. The curtains were drawn back to reveal tables draped in white linen and greenery, and servers moved gracefully among the guests, offering appetizers and wine.

The familiar chatter and laughter of my friends filled the air. Wendy, her arm linked with Rhys's, caught my eye and gave me a small, knowing smile. I smiled back, feeling a rush of affection for them both.

As I took in the twinkling lights and candles, I felt as though I were in my own personal snow globe—one I would treasure for years to come. I heard snatches of laughter and saw glimpses of people I loved—Belle in animated conversation with Ellie, Peter pulling out Lucy's chair—but it was all a gentle, joyful blur.

At some point, Dave's hand found mine again. "Ready?" he asked softly.

I nodded, and he led me toward the center of the dance floor. The crowd quieted as the musicians began to play the unmistakable opening notes of "Unchained Melody."

When Dave gave me a small, playful bow and then pulled me gently into his arms, I placed my hand on his shoulder, and felt his other hand pressed firmly but gently at my waist. The singer's voice filled the barn, and Dave's gaze met mine, his dark eyes shining in the candlelight.

"Can you believe this?" I whispered.

Pulling me a little closer, he said, "Every second of it."

My cheek against his shoulder, I let myself breathe it all in. "I'm so glad I walked into that cocktail party," I murmured, half to myself.

Dave chuckled softly. "So am I. Though I had to work awfully hard to convince you I wasn't going anywhere."

A smile tugging at the corners of my mouth, I lifted my head to look at him. "Persistence has its rewards."

When the final notes faded away, Dave pressed his forehead to mine. "You know," he whispered, "you never did give me a grand romantic declaration."

I laughed softly. "Oh, hell, I love you."

He grinned, pulling me into another slow spin, even though the music had stopped. "That's my Leta."

As we came to a gentle stop, Dave brushed his thumb over the back of my hand and smiled at me like I was the only person in the world.

And in that moment, with Dave's hand in mine and our friends around us, I realized I hadn't just found peace in the Cotswolds—I'd found a love I never knew I was looking for. A journey that had begun in sorrow had led me to exactly where I needed to be. Now, Dave and I would build a new life together, one day at a time.

The End

What's next for Leta & Dave?

Thank you for reading *Paintings, Puppies & Murder*. I hope you enjoyed reading about the wedding as much as I enjoyed writing about it. If you've grown attached to Leta, Dave, and their opinionated pets, you'll love their first adventure as newlyweds.

A fresh start, a seaside festival, and a very inconvenient corpse.

Find out what married life holds for Leta and Dave in *Legacies, Lies & Murder*—Book 1 of the Prentiss & Parker Cozy Mysteries.

Love coastal cozies? Join my newsletter for an exclusive preview of *Legacies, Lies & Murder* plus photos of Cornwall and other subscriber-only goodies.